"You talk as if I'm some sort of siren!"

Eve went on, knowing he'd never believe her. "Really I'm only—"

"We know what kind of woman you are, Eve." He approached her slowly. "Gentle, unsophisticated, comradely and clever. Sit down while we discuss what I should do to get even."

He was like a stranger, ruthless, cruel, vindictive, but Eve still loved him. "And what punishment do you reckon fits my behavior?" she asked, shattered by his deadly anger.

"Marriage—with me," he replied calmly. "If I give your brother the interview it would have to be on the understanding that you are to be my wife."

His wife! The thought filled Eve with both rapture and desolation. As an act of vengeance, Rydal was tying her to him for life—or until he tired of her....

These books may be available at your local bookseller.

Don't miss any of our special offers. Write to us at the following address for information on our newest releases.

Harlequin Reader Service
P.O. Box 52040, Phoenix, AZ 85072-2040
Canadian address: P.O. Box 2800, Postal Station A,
5170 Yonge St., Willowdale, Ont. M2N 6J3

Night of the Beguine

Roumelia Lane

Harlequin Books

TORONTO • NEW YORK • LONDON
AMSTERDAM • PARIS • SYDNEY • HAMBURG
STOCKHOLM • ATHENS • TOKYO • MILAN

Original hardcover edition published in 1985
by Mills & Boon Limited

ISBN 0-373-02745-1

Harlequin Romance first edition February 1986

CHAPTER ONE

COCONUT trees, sea grapes and flowering shrubs edged the crescent of pale sand. The sea, stretching to azure, pristine horizons, softened from deep blue and turquoise on the incoming swell to a cool translucent green at Eve's feet. Sandals in hand she paddled girlishly, smiling to herself at how easy it was to imagine oneself entirely alone with only the trade winds singing through the palms and the birds and wild-life contributing to that deserted feel with their uninhibited songs and calls in the undergrowth. If she was ever destined to be shipwrecked, her grey-green eyes danced as they scanned the scene, she hoped it would be in a spot like this.

Kicking up the spray so that it sometimes caught the hem of her cotton dress, she wondered idly why Rex hadn't been in a mood to accompany her on her paradisical stroll. Where else would one find blossoms as big as tea trays, ferns growing so tall they brushed the sky, and a peace that seemed age-old and unmarred by the contemporary pace and bustle of the outside world? She inhaled the scent of the breeze and sun-dried coral and thought lovingly of her brother lounging at the wheel of the car while she indulged her fancies for exploring cut-off beaches. In more ways than one he was an enigma to her.

Why, for instance, had he suddenly dropped in on her, after a long absence, at her rooms in Ingledene with plans for a holiday on Martinique all mapped out, and unwilling to take no for an answer? Martinique! Somewhere on the other side of the world; the French West Indies! Well of course she couldn't go! Major

Llewellyn, the elderly proprietor of the newsagents and tobacconists she worked at in the high street, would certainly not agree to her taking two, let alone three weeks off without notice, especially around Christmas time. Yet here she was. Rex had talked her into it. But she still had qualms about her job when she got back, and what she would do, in case of dismissal, to support herself and pay the rent of her rooms overlooking the village green. She wasn't like Rex. She hadn't gone out into the world and made it sit up and take notice of her.

Orphaned at an early age, she and her brother had been cared for by an aunt at Ingledene vicarage. But at eighteen Rex had grown impatient with rural life and the doting affections of a pig-tailed fifteen-years-old sister, and left for London. Always sure of himself he had done well in his chosen profession, journalism, rising rapidly from cub reporter to the ranks of important news coverage. Now at twenty-seven, he was making something of a name for himself as a columnist with a difference. He tracked down the elusive in the world of business, politics and society circles, securing personal interviews with recluse types while others in his field got no further than penetrating the outer screen of spokesmen for the individual currently in the public eye.

Over the years, and having a variety of newspapers to peruse through in the sleepy high street shop, Eve had followed her brother's career avidly. She sometimes felt that his methods were a little slick; often he was accused by other journalists of resorting to bribery and implicating current girl friends in his quest for news, and she was saddened by a hard core he seemed to be developing in his style, noticeable on the infrequent occasions that he dropped in to see her at Ingledene. But as her only close family he was still the most important man in her life.

When her uncle had died the clergy had installed a new

church head at the vicarage and Eve had moved out with her aunt to rooms above the local bakery. Though she had been on her own for some time now it was not through timidity that she chose to stay in Ingledene, so much as a lack of desire to move further afield or sample city life. Now look at her! She laughed briefly to the heavens. Eve Bowen, who had never been further than Brighton Beach and a day trip to the Belgian coast, paddling in tropical waters and viewing real live coconut palms!

With Rex extolling the delights of basking in the warm Antilles sunshine while England shivered, and dining alongside coral shores where flying fish rise at dusk Eve had succumbed to the madness of dropping everything in her secure, if mundane, little world to accept his invitation. They had flown in yesterday and booked in at a modest little *pension* in downtown Fort-de-France. Rex's finances apparently didn't run to the luxurious establishments in the Pointe du Bout hotel area across the bay. That was another thing which caused her a momentary pang of concern, but she quickly brushed it aside. One thing she could be sure of, Rex was thoroughly worldly and he always knew what he was doing. If he said that she needed a holiday away from the drizzle of an English winter, why dwell on the idiocy of it? Why not take advantage of his generosity and leave it at that? As he had pointed out there was more to life that clinging to old ways in a drowsy Sussex village. And perhaps he was right. Already she was deeply affected by the beauty of her new surroundings and the spell of *Madinini*, The Island of Flowers as the Indians had called Martinique.

On this their first day out in a hired car Rex had driven her through banana plantations to this wild stretch of coastline. She hadn't asked why he had chosen the Atlantic side of the island where most of the beaches were accessible only by boat, as opposed to the

Caribbean side throbbing with Martinique life. She supposed it was with a desire to take things slowly at first by enjoying what nature had to offer on the island. And that was just what she proposed to do. Rex had stopped on the road here and she had immediately fallen in love with this crescent of beach tucked away between twin, crumbling headlands. He hadn't shared her enthusiasm for exploring but had willingly given her a hand over the steep, tumbled rocks towards the powdery white sand. Now she was on her own and she had some minutes at least to wander where she pleased.

Tallish and slender she kept to the edge of the waves and decided to do the whole stretch of beach in this way, returning later alongside the undergrowth where she should be able to pick some of the lush flowers for her room at the Pension Desirade.

Leaving the shelter of the headland her mid-length brown hair, gold-streaked in the sun, was soon fingered into awry waves by the tropical breeze. The smooth skin of her bare arms and legs, she noticed, was paler than the sand beneath her feet. She was wondering as she idly watched a rainbow-tinted crab scuttle out of her path, if she would end up as mahogany-coloured as the other tourists she had seen in Fort-de-France, when a disturbing sound came to her ears; that of barking dogs. They were not just ordinary barks but ferocious, hysterical yelps, and they sounded, Eve realised suddenly, disconcertingly close.

Before she had time to think two huge shapes burst out of the undergrowth some distance away and hurled themselves towards her scattering the sand in all directions with their flailing paws and snarling, incensed approach.

All at once Eve's day-dream of shipwrecked shores and romantic castaways dissolved behind a blood-chilling close-up of drooling jaws and bared fangs of creatures who belong only in nightmares. Riveted at the speed with which these Stygian brutes had reached her she could only stare paralysed into their hate-filled yellow eyes. Reared on hind legs she could feel their snapping hot breath on her skin then a shout from somewhere in the undergrowth had them lowering to all fours and dropping back an inch or two.

A further shout from a native attendant in white drill, whom her distracted gaze had caught sight of, and growlingly and distrustfully the dogs obeyed his whistle to retreat. Beside him another man, the first to appear from out of the undergrowth, came loping towards her. He reached her almost as quick as the nightmare apparitions had done. She saw that he was tall and well-built. He looked at her with enquiring eyes of the most chilling blue.

It had all happened so fast the shock was only now upon her. The result was that her legs gave way beneath her and her eyelids lowered to shut out the horrifying memory of those drooling fangs. She had never fainted in her life but the man confronting her must have thought she had sunk into a deep swoon for before she had time to recover herself she felt the touch of strong impersonal hands through her thin dress as she was gathered into equally strong, impersonal arms.

Why she didn't protest she couldn't explain. Perhaps it was a desire not to appear foolish by struggling in the stranger's grasp. A quick glance through fractionally raised lids as she was transported towards the trees told her that the attendant had disappeared and so had the dogs.

Gripped against the hard frame, feeling the rhythmic stride, the strength of a man who was completely unknown to her, surging close to her own limp body, brought the warmth of embarrassment to her cheeks. Yet it was not unpleasant resting against the broad chest, wrapped in an aura of the man's own particular male fragrance, the lingering traces of aftershave, laundered shirt and good quality cigarettes.

There was an opening in the undergrowth which she hadn't noticed in her dreamy surveyance of the coral strand earlier; a path which led to what looked like a beach bungalow in a small clearing. It was low-roofed and of solid, rustic design. The interior too, which she glimpsed through flickering lashes a few seconds later, was rustic, although cushioned loungers, rugs on the gleaming tiled floors and lush, potted plants gave it a mellow kind of luxury.

Beside latticed windows emitting the green light from the forest outside she was deposited impersonally on a beach-striped divan. She was careful to keep her eyes firmly closed while she was being lowered. For some reason it was unthinkable to open them now and look straight into those arctic blue ones she had glimpsed momentarily before sinking to the sand on the beach.

Her heart thudded uncomfortably as she lay vulnerably stock still. What would happen now? Could she plausibly sit up and say there was no need for further clinical concern? Before she could decide what to do one of those firm hands came under her head and a glass of foul-smelling liquid was put to her lips. She coughed and grimaced as the fiery mixture ran down her throat and was thinking of half-raising herself when a deep, sarcastic voice sounded in her ears, 'I know a pair of Dobermen guard dogs on the offensive are a pretty grisly sight but they've gone back to their posts now so it's quite safe to open your eyes.'

Crimson-cheeked she knew then that he had been aware all along that her semi-comatose state was not altogether genuine. In her humiliation she swung her bare feet to the ground and replied stiffly, 'How dare you let such animals roam loose on the beach! I could have been torn to shreds. I've a good mind to report the incident to the authorities as soon as I get back to Fort-de-France.'

Immediately she knew that this was not the wisest

attitude to adopt with the man facing her. From where she sat he towered menacingly his blue eyes ice-chips as he drawled, 'Cut out the act and let's get to the point. This is private property and you knew it when you sneaked in here.'

Private property! Eve felt her humiliation deepening. 'I did not sneak in here,' she retorted tremblingly. 'I simply walked around the headland and there were no signs as far as I could see, advising me against it.'

'It's a precipitous stroll.' The sarcasm was now incisive. 'The rocks and boulders there have been deterrent enough up to now for wandering busybodys. Why not come out with it. You were assisted into an area that is well known on the island to be taboo, and you didn't come to admire the conch shells.'

Eve's first thoughts were to keep Rex out of the scrape she had landed herself into. 'I may not have come off very well with your unwelcoming beasts,' she quivered, 'but I can assure you I'm not exactly senile. I found the rocks no problem. I was keen to explore what I thought was a deserted stretch of beach . . .'

'And you didn't risk cricking an ankle or breaking a bone or two to get to try and see me.'

His acrimonious statement puzzled her. 'You flatter yourself, don't you?' Smarting at his attitude she smiled icily. 'I can't imagine anyone going out of their way to meet you, Mister . . .'

'And *of course* you don't know my name.' His sneer—one couldn't call it a smile—was laced with such cynicism Eve felt her throat flush, even though she was angrily perplexed at his contempt.

'I don't know your name, and I haven't the least inclination to find out,' she snapped. 'I was enjoying the first day of my holiday here on Martinique until I had the misfortune to trespass on your . . . your . . . private kingdom. But believe me you will fade as quickly from my mind as your disagreeable wolf-hounds the moment

I get out of this place. Now, if you've finished the interrogation . . .'

She rose with the intention of marching on her way only to find, to her surprise and horror, that her body offered her about as much support for her haughty withdrawal as an empty sack. She would have gone sprawling weakly had not the man with the glacial blue eyes caught her in his arms. 'A combination of shock and the drink I gave you,' he said with a curt grin. 'Whether you like it or not you'll have to lie prone until the effects of both have worn off.'

As her legs were like rubber she was forced to rely on his strength until she was once again draped back admidst the cushions on the divan. He straightened then to his formidable height and looked down at her with what she felt, having the temerity to meet his appraisal, was the mildest suggestion of a thaw in his demeanour. 'If it's true what you say, that you're a holidaymaker out on your first trip,' he spoke in his clipped way, 'then you would be well advised in future to study your guide literature before blundering into places where strangers aren't welcome.'

'Don't worry!' With what heat she could muster she replied, 'The next time I go out exploring a beach I'll make sure it's well and truly "public" first.'

'That would be a pity.' His hard mouth quirked. 'There are many beautiful spots unspoilt by tourism in Martinique, and not all are owned by unsociable Englishmen.'

So he could be human. While she was churlishly noting this he added, 'When you have rested I'll escort you back the way you came. Meanwhile I'll take the swim I planned before your er . . . wayward arrival into my grounds.'

I'm just as sorry as you are that I set foot here! Though she was tempted to voice her thoughts aloud she refrained. After all, he was making an effort to be polite, and he had offered her the use of his divan.

He disappeared through a doorway along a tiled passageway. He must have changed and left by another exit for a few minutes later she heard him making his way down to the beach. In the silence of the room the impact of her rather disturbing adventure turned her insides hollow. She was assailed by a fresh wave of weakness which had nothing to do with fearsome guard dogs and tranquillising drinks. But for the first time her mind was free to pursue another train of thought. Where was Rex? It must be more than half an hour now since he had left her at the headland. Why hadn't he come to see what had happened to her? Surely he had heard the furore with the dogs?

As no answers offered themselves to this baffling line of conjecture she gave in to the droopy feel of her eyelids. But even with eyes closed the image of the man she had just clashed with was strong in her consciousness. Like the run-back of a film the whole incident was impressed on her memory so that she could see him still as he had loped towards her on the beach, and she was seeing him now as he had towered over her on the divan. His features were rough hewn and far from handsome, but there was something brooding and powerful in his personality that went far deeper than looks . . .

She must have sunk into a slumber for there was a twilight ambience about the room when she opened her eyes. A glance at her watch told her that she had slept for over an hour! Quickly she sat up thankful to find that the giddiness had left her.

She pushed into her sandals which had been placed nearby and was on her feet when a shadow fell across the passageway. 'I came in earlier but you were . . . what shall we say? Out for the count.' Drily giving the impression that he had things to do other than wait around for lone women trespassers who ran up against his guard dogs then succumbed with the fright of it in his beach bungalow, the man with the austere countenance moved in. His springy dark hair was damp after his swim and was that a spark of leniency in his regard as he surveyed her? 'You're looking better,' he said. 'I take it you're ready to leave?'

'More than ready,' she affirmed stiltedly.

'Right.' She couldn't be sure but she thought the spark in the blue eyes seemed more pronounced. 'I'll see you off the grounds myself. There's no need for anyone else to be involved in this.'

As they went out and along the path towards the beach Eve wondered who he could be referring to with his last remark; the attendant who appeared to be in charge of the guard dogs? Or were there other types in the background employed to protect the man's privacy?

The sand was soft and powdery alongside the undergrowth. She viewed the crescent of beach and violet sea through different eyes now. The giant hibiscus, orchids and poinsettia were as devastatingly lovely as ever but the magic of the place had changed subtlety in a way she couldn't describe since she had discovered the owner of the pocket paradise.

His hand on her upper arm, impersonally assisting her over the uneven ground he asked, 'Do you think you'll make it okay round the headland?'

'I'm sure I shall have no difficulty,' she replied coolly, stifling her own personal doubts on the matter as they neared the craggy incline. 'My car is parked on the road so you can safely wash your hands of me once I'm over the rocks.'

She had no worries about Rex. Their transport was adequately screened behind the jutting outcrop. But the rubble looked considerably more formidable than it had done earlier in the afternoon when she had gaily accepted her brother's assistance to scale it. Just the thought of doing it alone now made her steps falter.

The strong hand on her arm seemed firmly intent on steering her off the premises regardless, then at the last moment it relented. 'It might be wiser to avoid further problems like cracked knee-caps and doubly incumbent trespassers,' he eyed her and the outcrop ironically and veered slightly. 'There's a small gate buried in the undergrowth somewhere along here. It's not officially in use but I reckon we can waive the rules this once.'

'I assure you there's no need to make special concessions on my account,' Eve smiled stiffly. He couldn't wait to see the back of her. But then the feeling was mutual.

'As a newcomer to the island, Miss . . .?' he gave her a hand over a clump of wild nutmeg.

'Bowen,' she supplied woodenly. 'Eve Bowen.'

'As a newcomer to Martinique, Miss Bowen, a word of advice in your ear. Any hospitality that's offered, no matter how small, be sure to show your appreciation. The islanders are a simple people but proud.'

'Are you saying I should be indebted to you for life for yours?' she asked smoothly.

His implacable blue glance took on a gleam. 'I seem to recall that I will linger no longer in your mind than your experience with my disagreeable wolf-hounds, once you have left.' She felt that he was teasing her in a granite kind of way.

'I'm sure your islanders will agree that the sort of reception you lay on for visitors is not the ideal way to win friends and influence people,' she replied in similar vein.

They had reached the gate. Excessively masculine, in pale tailored slacks and dark shirt he slackened his big frame into something resembling a bow. The gesture, she sensed, was as far as a man like him was prepared to go in the way of an apology. 'I'm sorry about the dogs,' he said, managing a caustic grin.

'And I for trespassing.' She couldn't help it if her own smile was a little ungracious. 'I shall take care to exclude this section of the island from any future touring itineraries.'

'My estate includes only the beach and the acres between the two headlands. I wouldn't want to deprive you of scenery generally around this way.' He opened the gate after a minor battle with entwined vines and the wiry branches of flowering shrubs, and suavely stood aside for her to pass through. 'It will take you about three minutes to reach the road.' He nodded into the green gloom. 'Enjoy your holiday, Miss Bowen.'

'Thank you, I intend to, Mister. . . .' Already on her way she glanced back but he had disappeared, hidden by the thick undergrowth as he retraced his steps along the beach.

Pausing momentarily it occurred to her that he hadn't told her his name. But then she had said that she was not remotely interested in finding out. Nor was she. At least . . . As she trod the forest path out to the road she did not put the man with the inflexible manner out of her mind as quickly as she had professed she would do.

The feel of his arms as he had transferred her from the water's edge to his beach bungalow was something equally difficult to eradicate from her memory and she found herself wondering, despite the fact that she had vowed she wouldn't give him another thought, who he was, and why he was living here isolated even from the islanders.

CHAPTER TWO

IN the glow of the lowering sun Rex was reclining, his feet on the dashboard, reading a paperback when she got back to the car. At the sight of her he hurriedly stuffed the book in the compartment and straightened.

'That's the last time I'll go wandering willy-nilly off the beaten track on *this* island,' she said grimly, sliding into her seat.

'What happened?' His eager expression floored her.

'What happened?' she echoed edgily. 'I was set upon by two very unfriendly guard dogs. It turned out that the idyllic half-moon beach that you were anxious for me to enjoy at close quarters is owned by an arbitrary Englishman with the same affection for strangers as his dogs. And incidentally,' she eyed her brother crossly, 'what happened to *you*? You must have heard the fuss with the howling beasts, and I've been gone ages. Why didn't you come to see what was going on?'

'Never mind that now,' Rex brushed her ill-humour aside, his eagerness coming over so strong it brought a pink flush to his fair features. 'Just tell me what transpired . . . what you've been doing all this time.'

'Mainly sleeping off the effects of bared fangs at close quarters and unpleasant property owners equally menacing,' she said drily. Not beginning to understand his sharp interest in her adventure she related all that had taken place adding, 'And now perhaps you'll tell me why you've been sitting here with your feet up when you knew I should have been back from my brief stroll hours ago?'

With an absent grin Rex replied, 'I wanted to see how you made out.'

If Eve had been puzzled before at her brother's attitude she was hotly mystified now, but before she could blurt out any kind of protest he was suddenly all action. 'Look. We can't talk here,' he said, starting up the car. 'Let's get back to town. I'll explain everything at the pension.'

As they tore away Eve could only go on staring at her brother's pleased features in the dumb hope that she would find some answers there. Why *couldn't* they talk right here? It was a public highway, wasn't it? And why was he in such a hurry to quit the vicinity after calmly sitting it out while she extricated herself from a decidedly tricky situation? But the thing which nagged deep in her consciousness was his remark *I wanted to see how you made out*. What had he meant by that?

She hardly saw the rugged peaks and fertile valleys on their return trip, but once back in the ebb and flow of Fort-de-France's noisy traffic, the incident of the afternoon began to take on an unreal quality in her mind as though the normality of city life had put it in its proper perspective. Well what was it after all but the mistaken entry into private property? And probably Rex was having a little joke with her because he had half suspected that she might be trespassing.

It was easy to lull herself into a more comfortable mood weaving among the dusky islanders crowding the narrow streets, and later sitting beneath the flowering bougainvillaea shading from purple to red to palest lavender on the tiny patio of their street *pension*. Until she saw Rex's business-like smile over their drinks.

'I could kiss you for being such a clever young woman this afternoon, Eve,' he said, rapidly going into a huddle with her at the table. 'By the way, can you describe the man who came to your assistance on the beach and carried you to the bungalow?'

'He was big, a bit hatchet-faced and very withdrawn.' Eve couldn't think how she had been clever.

'That's him.' Rex took a long pull from his glass and set it down again with satisfaction.

'That's who?' She could only stare at him in wonderment. 'You don't mean to say that ... you know him?'

'Don't you?' Her brother tilted an eyebrow. 'After being closed up with him for some considerable time in his beach house.'

'We didn't get round to introductions,' she said, straight lipped, not liking the slant he was putting on the incident. 'The man clearly made it known that he would not tolerate intrusions on his privacy, and I was concerned only with leaving him to his precious strip of beach at the earliest possible moment.'

'Nevertheless,' Rex's smile sloped mysteriously, 'you stayed the pace for much longer than I had hoped, and that, my sweet, is going to be useful during our session on Martinique.'

'Session?' she echoed slightly over a thread of uneasiness at her brother's odd behaviour. 'You make it sound like some kind of work trip instead of a holiday.'

'Let's say it's a little of each.' He reached for cigarettes, lit up after she had turned his offer of one down and blew the smoke out towards the colourful passers-by beyond the forecourt. He asked then, almost casually, 'Ever heard the name Rydal Grantham?'

'No.' Eve gave a disinterested reply. 'At least ...' something flitted across her mind '... only vaguely. I think I saw it, an item in the local paper recently when I was counting them out for the evening delivery.'

'You think!' Rex sighed in exasperation. 'My dear rusticated sister. You've been buried so long in that Brigadoon hamlet of yours, you're in danger of losing track of world events. Every news media in the U.K. and Europe is jumping with speculation about your "item" in the village press.' He heaved in a breath and explained with a patient grin, 'Rydal Grantham is one of the top aircraft designers in Great Britain. He recently walked out of a board meeting in London and disappeared. There's talk that the French government are buttering him up. The Americans would also like him to design for them. But our Mister Grantham is saying nothing of his future plans, nor,' her brother paused to give effect to his words, 'does any of my fellow newshounds know where he is.'

'Rex.' Eve fiddled with her glass the uneasiness burgeoning inside her. 'You know this kind of talk means nothing to me. It's your job, I realise that, but it is rather over my head. I came here for a holiday, not to listen to you clueing me up on . . . on world events.' She tried to inject a note of humour into her voice.

'Just the same, Eve, you're going to hear me out.' Suddenly Rex was grimly serious. 'Rydal Grantham is on this island. You met him this afternoon. And I want a personal interview with him before I leave.'

Eve was transfixed, but at the same time she experienced a mild wave of relief. 'Then surely all you have to do is inform him that you are here,' she said steadily.

'Dear naïve little sister.' Rex twisted a smile. 'The ingenuity I used to track him down to this unlikely spot on the other side of the world may have given me an exclusive—as we call it in the business—that the best brains on the news scene would give their right arm to possess, but I can't just go and knock on his front door expecting an invite. A man like that takes care to keep himself well-screened from the public, and the dogs you encountered will probably give you some idea of Grantham's opinion of pushy journalist types like me.'

At the best of times Eve had trouble coping with her brother's shrewdness of mind. Now, curiosity uppermost in her own, she asked, 'Then what do you propose to do?'

'*I* don't intend to do anything.' Rex eyed her in that

odd way then became intense again. 'It turns out that Grantham has had the property you ... er ... stumbled on to this afternoon for some time. Martinique is French to the back teeth so it could be he's here because of Gallic sympathies. On the other hand, the island is always well populated with visiting Americans so maybe the yanks are courting him. And why did he walk out of that board meeting? What happened to get his back up? Is he really a floating golden proposition to the world's top aircraft concerns, or can the U.K. still count on his genius for designing? These are questions I need the answers to, Eve, and you can get them for me.'

'I?' She blinked and laughed to lighten the peculiar tension in her throat. 'You must be suffering from an overdose of Caribbean sun, Rex. I'm not a journalist.'

'That's the best part of it.' He smiled his queer smile. 'You're neither clever nor worldly and I'm staking my reputation on a hunch that I have that you're just the girl for the part. After all he didn't throw you out on your ear, did he?'

'What's that supposed to mean?' she asked shakily.

'It means, my love, that you've broken the ice with him. Now all we have to do is arrange a second meeting—accidentally of course—and the chances are, as you stayed the pace with him for the best part of two hours this afternoon, it could be the start of a beautiful friendship.'

'Rex,' she protested beneath her breath even though the other tables in the forecourt were empty, 'you must be out of your mind ...' It was some moments before she could get a grip on herself to ask tightly, 'Am I to assume that you deliberately planned that incident at the beach? You knew it was private property yet you let me go in—even encouraged it—in the hope that I'd run into your ... your news scoop?'

' 'Fraid so, Sis.' Her brother grinned hardily and

shrugged. 'All right, I've got lady friends in the business who would willingly step into the breach for me. In fact they'd get quite a kick out of leading a big time recluse on for a story. But Grantham's different. He's cagey. He's also known to be ruthless with those who deceive him. He'd see through one of my slick, smooth-talking females in a minute. You're not like that, Eve. You're simple and warm-natured. He's not going to be on his guard with you. And that's when they start to talk.'

'I must be simple to believe all you said back home about my needing a holiday in the sun.' She bent the meaning of his words wryly.

'You were my only hope in a tricky situation.' His grin broadened. 'I had to talk you into it. Look.' He became serious again. 'For the past few years our designing expert has lived and worked in that strata of society denied to all but the very rich. He's used to being surrounded by beautiful, sophisticated women. You're not beautiful, Eve, and you're not worldly wise, but you've got something the others haven't got. You've a homespun dignity and a purity in your smile.'

She allowed her lips to form into warped humour. He was right in one sense. She hadn't inherited the good looks of the family. They had all gone to Rex. With his fair hair and baby blue eyes and sharply handsome features he could wring out almost any favour from the opposite sex—but not from her.

'Whatever I've got I'm taking home with me,' she said flatly. 'You may have tricked me into meeting a prospective victim of yours, Rex, but I wouldn't dream of letting it happen a second time.'

'Now wait a minute.' Her brother's expression hardened. 'Let's not forget who owes who what. It cost me a pretty penny to bring you out here and accommodation, even at *pension* rates, on the island is not cheap.'

'I don't have to stay three weeks. I can go home

tomorrow.' She set her glass down carefully. 'In fact I prefer to.'

'Don't forget I've got your passport.'

She looked at him with widening eyes. 'You wouldn't withhold it?'

'I'd do anything to get this story, Eve. Don't you understand?' Feverishly he gripped her hands across the table. 'This one job could set me up big in my profession. Without it I could go on being a second rate journalist all my life.' He clamped his teeth. 'I've done weeks of groundwork to get this far. I'm not going to let it slip through my fingers now.'

Eve lowered her gaze at his intensity. She felt her love for him surging through her at his touch. Rex was her brother. Her only kin in a big and lonesome world. Surely it was up to her to help him if she could. Even though his request sickened her. 'What would I have to do?' she asked faintly.

'Just be yourself,' Rex replied eagerly. 'I'll attend to the details.'

'You talked about a personal interview.' She fiddled with her glass.

'I was being optimistic.' Her brother let his smile slide. 'Grantham would never consent to see me. But you can be my go-between for the information I need. I can package it just as attractively for the public. And it's going to be the scoop of the year, make no mistake about that . . .'

A go-between, Eve experienced a feathering of disgust at the term. But wasn't she being over-sensitive? After all the man her brother had set his sights on to boost his career was more or less a total stranger to her. Up to this afternoon she hadn't known he existed. And when she returned to Ingledene he would cease to have any significance in her life. If Rex wanted her to pretend a passing friendship with such a man while she was on the island could there be any real harm in it?

One could tell oneself that these casual acquaintance-ships happened all the time in holiday places. Yet all her senses cried out against the idea.

'What if he doesn't talk?' She clutched at straws to rid herself of the onus that Rex had put on her. 'What if he doesn't say anything at all about his work?'

'He will.' Her brother beamed confidently. 'Every man likes to unload the weight off his mind once in a while. And there's nothing like a woman for providing a soothing audience.' At Eve's downcast expression he leaned in, 'Oh, come on, Sis! There's nothing dishonest in what I'm asking you to do. You'll actually be doing the public a service. News is a vital commodity in a free society. You'll simply be oiling the wheels for yours faithfully the one and only news ferret in these parts.'

Eve looked deep into his beseeching blue eyes and capitulated. 'All right, Rex. I'll do it,' she said unhappily before her mood changed to one of firmness. 'But one thing I want to make clear. When this so-called holiday is over I want to return to Ingledene and forget completely that I was ever involved in anything to do with your job.'

'Done!' he agreed, highly satisfied. Almost rubbing his hands he added, 'And don't forget I'm not just in this for the prestige. For a story like this I can get world syndication. And maybe your untrained, delicate ears are not familiar with the term so let's just say it could make me a very wealthy man.'

Eve directed her glance towards the street and the passers-by to hide her distaste. To the whisper of bare feet a tall dusky woman strode lithely along, a wooden tray of vegetables on her head. Behind her trotted a pint-sized carbon copy bearing a smaller burden. But it was not the moment to appreciate such endearing typicality. For his own ends Rex had launched her into a very dangerous situation this afternoon. But for the quick thinking of Rydal Grantham and his attendant she could have been seriously mauled by the guard dogs. He was also proposing to spy into the private and personal life of a man who had made it clear he wished to be left in peace.

If Rex wasn't her brother she would be tempted to get up from the table and show her contempt for his methods by walking as far away as she could from here. But *if* in her own case was a word sealing off her escape. She was committed now and for a while she would have to live with her distaste and her disillusionment at his ways.

Instead of rushing away she forced herself to show an interest in the remains of her glass. Rex, however, well content with their chat, rose energetically. 'You stay and enjoy the view,' he said offhandedly. 'I've got things to do.'

'Where are you going?' She looked up mildly panic-stricken.

'Just to do some scouting around.' He calmed her with his smile. 'It won't be easy getting through the local bodyguard Grantham employs, but I dare say the old brain-box,' he tapped his fair temple with a slim finger, 'will come up with something to get you two together.'

Wretchedly she watched him go, slim and lithe and almost carefree. Before disappearing into the shadows he added, 'Don't worry if you don't see me around for a while. I'll be working on it.'

Left with the twilight of evening and the reddening sky Eve was seized by a fresh bout of panic. What could she be thinking of to make herself available for such a plan! What in heaven's name did she, a village shop assistant, have in common with a world-renowned designer of aircraft! Why didn't she run after Rex and tell him here and now that she would have nothing at all to do with his dubious schemes, that she was going back to Ingledene even if she had to swim it! Why?

A numbness overtook her so that she had no clear answers to these wild thoughts. She could not explain a peculiar reluctance to stir from her chair. If a tiny voice in her head suggested that it was because she could not fully reject the idea of seeing Rydal Grantham again, she tremulously ignored it.

CHAPTER THREE

HUMMINGBIRDS flashed like jewels among the blossoms overhanging the waterfront. Along the palm-shaded Caribbean shore-line nets bobbed in wide arcs between the native boats. As fish leapt, fell glittering and leapt again, straw-hatted fishermen moved excitedly in their knife-prowed dug-outs. Closer at hand other Creole men of the sea rowed their boats up the shallow river mouth to peddle their catch.

At *Rivière Madame*'s crowded wall eager housewives leaned over, elbowing each other for space and the juiciest *anguille* or *oursin*. One tawny islander who had forgotten her shopping bag handed down her battered hat for her purchase of tuna and silvery *coulirou*. It was Monday, Planters day, when the country in French Martinique comes to town. Along with half the island Eve had wandered around the tiny cubicles which served as shops, stepping into Lilliputian hardware stores and discovering that barbers also sold ice-cream! Now she watched the scene at the harbour wall musing on the chuckles and wide white smiles of the Creoles as they did business. And for the first time since her arrival on this Windward Isle she felt almost smitten by the general good humour of its inhabitants.

It was two days since she had seen Rex. A whole weekend and nothing had transpired concerning his plan. Could it be, she dared to air the thought in her mind, that nothing would? He himself admitted that it was practically impossible to involve someone as closely protected from the public as Rydal Grantham in an everyday situation. Was he discovering that there was just no way to procure the information he desired?

29

She had spent two restless nights worrying over her part in the affair, but her spirits now began to rise by the second. Perhaps Rex would see that it was useless to pursue this bizarre idea of his. Maybe he would decide to cut his losses and return home immediately. Eve would be sorry to leave the island but she would also know a powerful relief that she hadn't been called upon to form a pseudo-friendship with a man whom she felt deserved honesty despite his formidable appearance.

Lighter of heart she turned back in the direction of the Pension Desirade. After lunch she might even take a stroll to the town park to view the white marble statue of Empress Josephine, the famed wife of Napoleon, who, according to local literature, was born here. All at once she was beginning to feel like a carefree holidaymaker.

Once indoors at the *pension* she removed her sun-hat and took the tiny cage-like elevator to her room. It was a fascinating apparatus. Travelling upwards in the meshwork lift shaft one could see the winding stairways and all the inner workings of the bijou hotel. Happily there was only three floors so there was no danger of suffering an attack of vertigo.

At the door of her room the first thing she noticed when she opened it was a white envelope which had obviously been slipped underneath. Curiously she picked it up and slit it open then seeing Rex's handwriting she smiled to herself. He had been a journalist for so long she supposed he couldn't help being mysterious. He wanted her to meet him at a tucked away *bistro* round the corner from the *pension*.

With a resigned gleam she replaced her sun-hat and set off to find the establishment whose name he had written down. He was no doubt feeling sheepish about the failure of his outlandish plot and wanted to edge round gradually to the subject of going home, over a pre-lunch aperitif.

The *bistro* was in fact half a block away from the *pension*. Narrow-fronted and garishly decorated she was on the point of passing it by until she spotted Rex at the last moment almost screened by a potted magnolia on the forecourt. Surreptitiously he gave her a wave and ordered her a drink and humouring him she also sat with her back to the street and the strolling townspeople. She could afford to take a lighter view of his introvert habits she told herself amusedly, now that, in this case, the horrid business of spying on strangers had come to nothing. She might even ask Rex if they could stay on a day or two simply as tourists. Martinique was a heavenly spot. She would like to see a little more of it before she left.

She was happily sipping her drink when something about her brother's tense attitude caught her glance. True, he was behaving in typical cloak and dagger fashion but that familiar eager light was in his eyes. And come to think of it there was nothing at all sheepish in his expression. When he spoke her heart sank like a stone.

'We're in business,' he said beneath his breath. 'Our friend the aircraft designer will shortly be leaving his island stronghold and I've worked out a nifty way for you two to run into each other.'

'Wh ... what are you talking about?' she asked dazed. 'I've had no word ... I mean, you've been gone so long I ... thought you'd given up this crazy idea of yours.'

'Honey.' His smile was patient. 'These things take time. I've been on the job ever since I left you. Spent two sleepless nights working out the strategy so that you bumping into your guard-dog rescuer a second time looks natural.'

'You don't seem any the worse for your lack of sleep.' She examined his glowing features morosely. 'In fact you appear to thrive on it.'

He laughed shortly then leaned in across the table out of view of the others on the forecourt. 'Now listen. We haven't got much time so here's what you have to do. Apparently Grantham is well-liked on the island. The Martinique calendar is littered with Saints days and he's promised to attend a festival of some kind over at Corobrier—that's a small fishing village north from here. A long-serving member of his household belongs to that locality or something. Anyway that doesn't concern us. What is important is that among other things he's going to present the prizes for the best piña colada.'

Eve could only blink. With a grin he explained, 'That's a frothy, frosty mixture of rum, cream of coconut, pineapple juice and crushed ice. And the secret is in the blending. It's a lot of nonsense but the natives enjoy this kind of thing. There'll be the usual free feast with singing and dancing and dressing up.'

'Perhaps I'm dense,' Eve said through stiff lips, 'but I don't see how . . .'

'Wait until you've heard the rest,' Rex continued in smiling undertones. 'I told you I've been working on it. I've been out to Corobrier and sized the whole thing up neater than the lay-out for a V.I.P. abduction. The piña colada presentation takes place on a kind of straw-covered dais on the beach. After that everyone will be thinking about food. As the guest of honour Grantham will wait until the locals have dispersed then make his own way to where the native buffet is laid out in the village clearing. Now,' Rex paused for effect, 'we come to the clincher or *clinching*, if you work it right.' He gave a muffled laugh. 'There's only one route through to the village feast area from the beach and that is along a grassy path between volcanic rocks, banana palms etc. When all is quiet in that region, you, my angel will be coming the other way on the pretext of leaving the pandemonium of the food jamboree for a little relaxing sea air and *voilà!*—as they say in these parts—the two of you will meet bang-on in a nice secluded rocky clearing.'

Swallowing her alarm at the idea Eve said feebly, 'It sounds awfully hit and miss.'

'It may sound it, but believe me, it's all been timed to the last second,' Rex said in his intense way. 'You'll catch the four o'clock bus from here which will get you to Corobrier by four forty-five. The festivities will be well underway by then and there will be enough going on for you to behave like the local-culture struck tourist. Grantham will be on the beach dais at five, doing his stuff. At five-thirty prompt, accompanied by a couple of village officials whom we can ignore, he will follow the rest of the villagers to the bean feast. All you have to do is time it so that you are on that path linking the village to the beach at exactly the same time that he is.'

Eve had paled because it could just possibly work. 'How on earth . . . can you know all this?' she asked in strangled tones. 'The man's movements . . . his time table?'

'That's my job.' Rex shrugged easily. 'Don't forget I've learned all the tricks of the trade and then some. Once I'd tapped the leak on Grantham's programme for the week the rest wasn't too difficult.' A certain pride in his eyes he reflected with amusement, 'You buy a so-called official a rum punch at his beach buvette. You praise the fishermen and their kids. The islanders are like children anyway, including those in charge of the festivities. And with a celebrity as important as Monsieur Grantham gracing their humble assemblée, they'll talk all day given the right openings. Lucky for you,' he returned to the present decisively, 'Corobrier is well off the beaten track for the average sightseer, so you'll have the place to yourself, so to speak. The bus will drop you off in the village. It's small enough not to get lost in but big enough to allow you to blend in with the crowd until the right moment.'

'I . . . I thought you said . . . something about a local bodyguard.' Still looking for a loophole to escape Eve rushed in to point out.

'He only employs them to keep nosey-parker press men like me off his back.' Rex grinned. 'As this is strictly a native occasion they're likely to remain in the background. They certainly won't be watching a banana path belonging to a Creole community. That leaves the coast clear for, er . . . shall we say an accidental confrontation. Two fellow expatriates, as it were, who have already met previously, you the inveterate tourist, him . . . well it should be the basis for renewing acquaintanceships, even if you both use the old stand-by of chatting about the weather at first.'

Eve had no stomach for her brother's satirical humour. It was true, she and Rydal Grantham had respectively thawed out to a point of passable politeness before they had parted on his beach, but that was no reason to suppose he would do anything but look through her, even on a lonely footpath. But Rex seemed to think otherwise. She could only hope that she was right and he was wrong and that she would return after the outing to tell him that nothing at all had happened. And that should put an end to his foolish dreams where the aircraft designer was concerned.

'Wh . . . when is the festival due to take place?' She forced out the words.

'Tomorrow,' Rex said breezily. 'You can get the bus for Corobrier down on the harbour front where the ferries tie up. After that it should go like clockwork.'

'Tomorrow!' she echoed aghast. She had hoped to have several days in which to school herself to the idea.

She was not, she admitted, displaying any great confidence for the task and irritably Rex lowered his chin to mutter between set lips, 'Now look, Eve, I've gone to a lot of trouble to set this thing up. I don't want you blowing it, remember.' She supposed she must have looked fairly green for after a moment he softened and his manner became more subdued. 'Do this for me, Sis, and I'll never forget you.' His boyish features were pleading. 'With a scoop covering someone as hot as Rydal Grantham my name will be made. I'll be able to state my own price as a columnist, to say nothing of other avenues the story's likely to open up for me. Tell me you won't let me down, Eve. The whole works depend on you.'

Torn as she was Eve had no doubts in her mind that with her, her brother came first. Left alone in the world while very young they had grown up very close especially in their juvenile years. She was not likely to forget that, or the fact that when he looked at her like this all opposition in her melted with her love for him.

Though her whole being rebelled at her part in the scheme he had mapped out she said unsteadily, trying to inject some semblance of resolve into her voice, 'Don't worry, Rex ... I'll ... do as you ask.'

'Great girl!' Rapidly his mood changed and he was breezy again. 'Now I've got to go. Do as you've been briefed and you've got nothing to worry about ...'

Alarmed Eve saw that he was making to rise. Before he could do so she grabbed his arm and mumbled with a surreptitious glance at the other tables. 'But ... what about lunch? And what am I going to do this afternoon? I thought we might ... well do a trip together or something.' She knew that any sightseeing now would stick in her throat but she was clinging to Rex because he was her only anchor in what had suddenly become a worry-fraught existence.

'I'll eat when I can. Got to keep the pot boiling on this thing. Amuse yourself as you like, but don't miss that bus tomorrow afternoon.' He eased himself from his seat, paid for the drinks with the smoothness of a happy-go-lucky tourist and moved off to become lost in the stream of passers-by.

Drowningly Eve watched him go. After a few moments she saw that there was nothing to do but follow suit and on shaky legs she made her way back to the Pension Desirade.

It was the longest afternoon and evening of her life. She spent the time hoping that an earthquake would occur, similar to the one that had struck Martinique at the turn of the century—or a tidal wave. Anything to prevent her from fulfilling her promise. But the following day dawned sparkling and tranquil and the only way through it, it seemed, was to adopt a kind of fatalistic attitude. After all she was keen to see the island and it would be an adventure travelling on a native bus. She could forget all about Rydal Grantham until five-thirty and with the feeling of being a genuine tourist even if she ran into him she could tell herself it had been merely in the course of following her own pursuits.

This practical outlook, as a way of soothing her nerves, was fine until the moment came to board the bus. In a blue linen dress which had seen many summers at the vicarage, her hair combed loosely, she may have looked composed and eager but inwardly she felt keyed-up and uneasy. Fortunately there was so much going on inside the bus that her natural curiosity and interest helped to dull the tension.

From the moment the plane had touched down on the island she had known the atmosphere was richer, more exotic. Africans, Asians, Indians and Whites of various origins had become absorbed and transformed into the fascinating culture known as Creole. And the patois of the noisy occupants of the local transport was intriguing to listen to and to watch as it contained a great deal of mime. Peppered with English, French and

Spanish words it was a pot-pourri of sound and signs known only to the native Martiniquais.

It seemed that half the relatives of Corobrier were determined to cram into the interior for the latter half of the festival in their home village. Eve had next to her an overflow of children from a family in the seat behind, a huge water melon, gift-wrapped in a basket resting obligingly on her knee, and a trussed-up cockerel obviously destined for the cooking pot flopping complainingly on the rack above her head. As the rest of the space in the bus was more or less taken up in the same way, and being so rickety a contraption one had to clutch at anything available when careening round some bend on a dirt road, it could not have been called an unamusing journey.

Eve was learning that Martinique was an island of lush green hills, mountains and magnificent flowering vegetation. From her window she viewed flamboyants, hibiscus, oleander and poinsettia, and along the forest wayside locust trees, papaya and custard apple mingled with the ubiquitous palms. Fields of sugar cane linked the villages and as the time wore on the uneasy knot inside her began to make itself felt again.

Alighting at Corobrier, with its frame houses set among seaside greenery, was not the ordeal she had expected. For one thing so many villagers had come to meet the bus that she had no worries about being seen leaving it. Also the whole place was thick with the native element it seemed unlikely that anyone of her own kind would go out of their way to visit such a local affair. However tourists were not unheard of in these out of the way places so, wearing a veneer of the inquisitive visitor, she steeled herself into plunging into the carefree atmosphere.

If she had come strictly to soak up local colour she would have considered the trip worthwhile. A steel band was hammering out tuneful calypsos in the coconut palm-lined square. In another section drums were going and dark-skinned dancers in dashing red headdress and waistcoats and flowered silk trousers were threshing evil-looking machetes. The garb of the thronging revellers was even more imaginative. The women wore ankle-length white cotton dresses whose decorative broderie anglaise borders were threaded with red ribbon. Sober enough, but these were topped by gorgeous satin waist-to-hip length ruffs in vivid emeralds, golds, hyacinth blues and rose pink. The men sported sparkling white cotton trousers, gay paisley patterned or flowered shirts and gold bracelets.

It was considered the thing to just dance with your partner whenever you had a mind to, and couples and even whole families held hands and jigged for the fun of it whenever the calypso beat was particularly infectious. There were other dancers too, those with grotesque giant heads painted with lurid smiles, waggling on plump diminutive bodies.

The smell of food cooking was everywhere, the most tempting aroma coming from the crawfish grills where the halved crustaceans lay toasting succulently. Creole fritters were, not unexpectedly, popular and there were smoked herrings flamed in rum and spicy black pudding to tempt the passers-by. But though Eve moved in the thick of the gaiety, past impromptu drum gatherings, stalls piled with strange twigs, herbs and potions, and chanting processions based on traditions that stemmed from African origins, she knew in her heart that it was useless to cling to the hope that she was the only one of her kind in this wholly West Indian, and not a little primitive setting. Rydal Grantham was there, she could sense it. Rex would not have made a mistake in something so vital to his own future well-being. He had spent considerable time and energy tracking down his prey and though she had temporarily fooled herself into believing otherwise she knew that there was not the remotest chance that he had got the wrong village, or the wrong day, or even the wrong man. Rex was too clever for that.

A nervous glance at her watch told her that it was already five-twenty. In ten minutes, *just ten minutes*, she would have to make her way along the path towards the beach!

She had viewed earlier the leafy clearing with the palm-thatched tables heaped with every known island delicacy and fruit for the traditional feast. And she had seen the start of the grassy route winding between huge dark rocks and banana palms, which led to the sea. But the thought of having to go back to this spot now filled her with unmitigated dread. She wanted to wring her hands. How could Rex do this to her? How could he see her as some kind of *femme fatale* when in truth she was no more than a homespun vicar's niece?

Torn by her promise to him she finally forced herself to return to the main scene of events. Everyone was gathering there. The beaten-earth space was crammed with merry-makers, their numbers swelled perhaps by enthusiasts from other villages. And it looked as though the *piña-colada* contestants had returned from the beach, for the path which had been thronged earlier with the coming and going of islanders was now deserted.

She stole another look at her watch and saw to her horror that she had only two minutes left before her carefully timed stroll to the sea. She stood rooted to the ground unable to move. The thought of Rydal Grantham preparing to start out just about now from the beach side froze her even further. What should she say when she ran into him? What would she *do*? She would give herself away in the first seconds with her idiotic sense of honesty and her hopeless naïveté. The din, the music, the laughter of the crowds did nothing to help her shrieking nerves. She stared in a petrified way towards the banana path then turned and buried herself in the press of bodies around her. She couldn't do it. No, *not even for Rex*. She had tried. She had got this far but she had known all along she was a poor choice for this kind of duplicity.

Hurrying, seeking refuge beyond the clamour, and out of sight of that dreadful path she found, at last, a quiet tree-shaded track. The houses on either side were deserted. Distracted and filled with anguish at her action—what would Rex say now?—she took to viewing the gingerbread domains as a way of obtaining a steadier frame of mind. Brightly decorated timber verandas overlooking vegetable strips and plots of anthurium. The corrugated tin roofs were painted a gay red except in some cases where renewed metal sections gave the effect of patchwork. They were colourful but humble dwellings and it was easy to see why their occupants had temporarily deserted them for all the fun in the village square.

Eve walked for some minutes round the fishing settlement without having any clear idea of where to turn next. Then she saw it. The bus for Fort-de-France just trundling into the mango clearing where it had set her down earlier. Of course! She was galvanised into action. That was what she must do. Get away from here as quickly as possible. Never before had her room at the Pension Desirade seemed such a haven of peace. All she wanted to do was hide there and forget that she had ever tried, for Rex's sake, to play the ingenuous enchantress.

The bus would stay a few minutes and there was certainly no rush of passengers for the return trip at this hour of the celebrations, but frantically she ran all the same. The atmosphere locally may be reaching a fever pitch of excitement but for her Corobrier had been just a nightmare and the sooner she left it behind the easier she would breathe.

She was running blindly, aware that a cross-section

of the track was coming up but caring less. As she approached a figure who appeared to be in something of a hurry also, shot into view from around the bend and strode straight into her path.

There was a collision. Bruised and breathless she was steadied against a big frame while an inclement blue gaze surveyed her. At first surprise and then recognition on his inured features Rydal Grantham drawled, 'Well if it isn't the indefatigable lady tourist on another gate-crashing expedition by the look of it.'

CHAPTER FOUR

Too robbed of breath to speak and weak from panic and shock that it should be him, of all people, she had careered into, Eve could only stand gasping. His glance taking in her over-brilliant grey-green eyes, her flying gold-spun hair and breathless parted lips he said, 'You're moving as if you're scared of something. What brings you to Corobrier anyway?'

'Sightseeing, what else?' She tried to sound flippant when she could finally croak out a reply.

'Then why are you frightened of the masks and the dressing up and the trading in magic potions and spells?' His lips curled. 'It's what you expected isn't it?'

'I'm not frightened,' she snapped. 'I just felt I wanted to . . . to . . .' flounderingly she finished, 'get away that's all.'

She wouldn't have believed it but momentarily his pitiless blue eyes did appear to have a harsh tolerance in their depths as he asked resignedly, 'Is this your first trip abroad?'

'As a matter of fact it is,' she acknowledged coolly, discounting her outing to the Belgian coast of course.

'Well at the risk of repeating myself,' his flicker of indulgence had lapsed a little grim, 'my advice is to stick with the rest of your holiday guests and make for the popular tourist spots. If you go on blundering on to private beaches and getting yourself in too deep with native shindigs you're likely to return home a darn sight more frazzled than when you came.'

Eve hoped he couldn't feel the wild thudding of her heart. She was filled with a frenzied desire to flee but his arms still held her. 'Look.' She struggled to sound

42

indifferent to his remark. 'I'm trying to catch the bus. Do you mind?'

His eyes followed her frantic glance in that direction but his grip showed no signs of slackening. 'I would have thought,' he considered, turning an ear to the laughter and clamour beyond the forest greenery, 'that as you've taken all the trouble to get here you would at least see the thing through.'

'I've seen all I want to thank you. Please, let me go.' She felt hopelessly trapped, held as she was against him.

He eyed her keenly. 'You're upset about something.' His voice had a steely inflexion, 'Has someone—one of the Creoles here—given you a bad scare?'

She shook her head blindly. 'I'm not upset. I'm not frightened. I simply want to go back to Fort-de-France.'

'I'm not sure,' he said with his maddening logic, 'if it's a good thing you going away with the wrong impression of one of these local affairs, like this. It could colour your whole visit to Martinique . . .'

'Thanks, but I think that's my concern. Now if you'll just——' She was trying to find a way out of his encircling arms when she heard the sound of the island contraption starting up, and before her eyes it trundled off and away belching exhaust fumes as it went. 'Now look what you've done!' she almost wailed. 'I've missed the bus and there probably won't be another for ages.'

'Not until late tonight, I wouldn't think.' He lowered his arms, nothing penitent in his shrug. 'As that one has left empty the transport operators are not likely to put themselves out sending another one until after the gaity's finished around midnight.'

'In that case I'll walk.' Eve bit back her desperation.

'Now wait a minute!' Before she could take a step something in his manner checked her. 'When I fished you out of the jaws of the guard dogs you were pretty far gone, but you didn't strike me then as being the hysterical type.'

Eve would have given anything to put on a blasé smile at his sharp observation. She realised, much to her quiet horror, that she was in danger of giving herself away with her fanatical desire to escape from him. Battling to tone her mood down she said unsteadily. 'Anyone can tire of calypso rhythms, coconut brews, and carnival effigies.'

'I agree.' His tight mouth sloped. 'I was just in the act of sneaking away myself. But then I've seen all this a hundred times before, whereas this is your first visit. A little early by normal standards to go stale.'

Eve could think of nothing to reply to this. She refrained from glancing covertly around for a bolt-hole and substituted a passive expression when inwardly she willed a miracle to happen, like another bus drawing up beside her. Over her thoughts the aircraft designer asked with a kind of inclement mockery, 'Aren't you curious to know why I'm here?'

'Not in the least.' She stifled a fresh bout of panic. She sensed his taut reaction.

'Okay, I know I gave you a rough time when I found you on my property,' he said drily. 'But that doesn't mean I don't have ... shall we say, a less charitable side for those who know me.'

It was barely noticeable among the flint, but of course Eve didn't voice her thoughts. Though she didn't invite an explanation as to why he was in Corobrier, and heaven knew she didn't need one, one was assertively forthcoming just the same. 'The couple who run my house on the island were born and bred in this village.' The man who had caught her against him in flight turned his glance towards the glow above the trees. 'For a while now it's been an understood practice whenever I'm on Martinique, that I enhance their popularity locally by presiding over their village festival. For some reason it gives them a kick if I put, what they regard as, a stamp of authority on the proceedings and this year among other things I've been dishing out prizes for the best folklore ballet group and most original *Rhum agricole*.' The suggestion of hardy humour flitted across his features. 'I was supposed to stay and reign over the monumental feast provided but the er ... committee, after enthusiastically sampling Planters Punch, coconut and guava mixtures etc., are too high by now to miss me. I was just discreetly making for my car when I ran into you here.'

Once again Eve could find no words. She dare not even flicker an eyelid in case she gave away her prior knowledge of his movements. The worst of it was he was eyeing her thoughtfully. 'I could give you a lift back to Fort-de-France ...' he mused aloud.

'No thank you.' She rushed her refusal.

'On the other hand,' he went on as though he hadn't heard, 'I wouldn't be doing my duty as a Martinique citizen if I let you leave Corobrier without first showing you that there is much to be admired in the local culture when the motives are understood.'

'I can assure you,' Eve reiterated, her nerves tightening further, 'my interest in island revels has sunk to nil.'

'Perhaps it needs but a little stimulation,' he said suavely. 'Shall we try? After all, you don't have a lot of choice do you? It will be dark shortly which cuts out your proposed hike, and I myself have just decided that I won't be driving back to Fort-de-France until late tonight.'

Eve contained her dilemma the best she could. Short of fleeing from him, which would only draw attention to her guilt, there was nothing she could do but remain here under his arbitraary gaze. Stiffly she commented, 'Isn't there a danger that I will cramp your style as the eminent celebrity, as it were?'

'On the contrary.' He shrugged off her argument.

'You might give it a boost. There is nothing the islanders like better than a European woman to appreciate their colourful ways.'

Eve gave him a condescending smile while trying to get a grip on herself. She was trapped. Trapped in a situation partly of her own making—or Rex's. Her plans to remove herself as far away as possible from her brother's underhand schemes had rather blown up in her face. But there was nothing she could do about it now.

She had noticed some time back two well-dressed Martiniquais hovering a few yards away along the track. As Rydal Grantham placed a hand on her elbow she saw him give them a nod, and relaxing they disappeared into the trees.

Far from simmering to a halt at dusk the merry-making at the fishing settlement of Corobrier seemed to take on renewed vigour with the coming of the dark hours. Rockets with blazing tails exploded into a myriad coloured stars over the sea, and limbo dancers were demonstrating their skill under low-slung rods of flames. And there was nothing the Creoles liked better it seemed than to move with the music; the steel band sound which reverberated under the coconut palms.

'Most of these French West Indian dances originated with the slaves.' Her escort guided her round a cock-fighting arena. Passing a plump matron swaying to the beat in her voluminous print he went on, 'Only in these country patron saint festivals do you see the true folk dances performed. This one is *le rose*, a slave woman's washing dance.' And further on where the beat of the goat skin drums was all insistent, 'These men are mimicking the tapioca graters.'

Though secretly intrigued by all he was telling her Eve said frigidly, 'It's not necessary to play the role of the indulgent guide on my account, Mister——' She saved herself in time from uttering what would have been a disaster. But her biting back his name must have looked like pure hesitation for he gleamed meditatively. 'That's right, I never did get round to introducing myself. My apologies, Miss Bowen, I'm known as Grantham. Rydal Grantham.'

She kept her glance carefully with the dancers in case he was looking for some kind of reaction. But she was just a rustic English village dweller and his prowess and fame on the other side of the Atlantic, despite Rex's professional excitement at having him for a subject, was lost on her.

Taking up from where they had left off he said, 'Look upon it as an educational tour. It will put you right for the rest of your stay on Martinique, and with my little efforts on behalf of the tourist board I may prevent you from starting off on the wrong foot on an outing, which you appear to be developing a penchant for.'

There was nothing for it after that but to regard herself as a holiday-maker, which first and foremost she was, and Rydal Grantham as a man politely out to help a lame dog, as it were.

In the flame-lit glow there was much to see in the settlement and now with the big Englishman at her side, speaking her own language, meticulously explaining to her the nuances of this machete brandishing act, and that swallowing tiny whole fish alive custom, her interest in the island culture deepened, beneath her cool reserve, to pure fascination.

On their tour they ran into members of the committee, ebony skinned fishermen with a flair for local politics who, at the moment, were more concerned with participating rather than organising the village fun and games. Smiles whiter than the sharks teeth necklaces they wore, they were ecstatic that Rydal Grantham their esteemed visitor, had seen fit to apply himself to enjoying Corobrier's humble efforts at merry-making. They fell upon Eve, leading her to their favourite foodstuffs and plying her with sea-urchin tarts and fritters, fried conch meat and codfish croquettes, and treating her as some prize possession of the big man's; an attitude which caused him some granite amusement and which she stoically ignored.

But she had to admit she was ravenous. She had hardly touched her lunch at the *pension*, being consumed with nerves at the thought of her trip to Corobrier. As they were now well into the evening the taste of those succulent slivers of grilled crawfish and hot tart of grated coconut were out of this world. She had to pull herself up at one point, recalling that she was here under false pretences, and that she should not at any time allow herself to feel relaxed with a man whom Rex had professional designs on. But it was difficult not to enjoy the food. And the aircraft designer, though of a hardbitten nature, made no secret of the fact that he was hungry too. This contributed, however hard she strove to maintain an aloof air, to a kind of distant companionableness between them. During their rounds of the festivities, with him relentlessly pointing out items of interest to her, she had developed a wooden way of conversing, and in this too now she was in danger of losing ground due to his easy style with his friends the Martiniquais, who of course included her in everything that was discussed though she didn't understand a word of their Creole.

However committee members are expected to circulate among their guests and after a while they reluctantly took themselves off to sample the local heady potions elsewhere. She was left alone with her broad-shouldered guide and a sea of munching, swaying, swigging islanders who were mainly intoxicated by the steel-band sound. Dressed in expensive white slacks and straw-coloured open-weave sports shirt her escort seemed to tower above the proceedings. For the sake of something to say she put in while finishing a papaya concoction, 'For an island this size they do rather go to town on their Saints' days, don't they?'

'You should see them at traditional carnival times,' she was told wryly. 'It starts at the beginning of the week with doudou dolls, pirate parades, spectacular floats ... Gets a bit riotous towards Mardi Gras— Shrove Tuesday—and distinctly frenzied later when the carnival king Vaval is burned in effigy at dusk. Dancing continues till dawn on Ash Wednesday, by which time everybody is on the point of collapse.'

'Sounds a little overwhelming,' Eve said reservedly. Her companion shrugged. 'Most tourists, like yourself, avoid the hysteria of the actual celebrations and join in the fun of the warm-up during the week or two before.'

Eve looked at the swaying shapes in the flame-lit glow and remarked, 'Perhaps they're getting in practice for approaching carnival time.'

'These people don't need to practice.' A tantalising fruit pie was reached for. 'It's in their blood. Their African ancestors lived by the rhythm of the drum. The rest comes as naturally to them as breathing.'

Eve felt that she should be taking more notice of what was going on around her and less of Rydal Grantham's chat, but he, case-hardened as he was, was not, it seemed, averse to bending with the wind, or in this case the party atmosphere. 'Coming next to their beautiful women and children,' he continued in much the same vein, 'the greatest pride of the Martiniquais must be their rum.'

Eve had heard a lot about the island's liquor industry but it was the first part of his remark which intrigued her. Ever since setting foot in Martinique she had been riveted by the beauty of the dusky-skinned women and young girls. No only did they possess smooth, classical features but their grace of style and movement must leave every foreign woman who visited the spot, green with envy. Why she herself should feel moved to comment wasn't clear to her but she found herself saying levelly, 'As you're almost an islander yourself, Mr Grantham, I wonder you haven't, by this time, acquired a Martinique woman for a wife.'

He appeared to weigh this remark almost with humour. 'I've never got that far.' He finished his pie in a neat bite. 'But I've been often tempted. For instance I was visiting the home of a friend in the hills a couple of days back. His daughter's a stunner. She came to twine her arms round my neck and kiss me on the lips when I was leaving. I was thoroughly smitten—and she's only three years old.'

Eve laughed. She couldn't help herself. But perhaps swelling her amusement was something like relief that the dusky damsel had turned out to be no more than a tot. Her eyes softly sparkling, her face faintly flushed, she was suddenly aware that the austere blue gaze across from her was studying her with something like steely laughter in it too. 'You know,' the man who made aeroplanes said deeply, 'that's the first time you've let yourself go all evening.'

She lifted her shoulders blushing an little. 'I must be smitten by the party atmosphere.'

'Is that what it is?' he said drily. And taking her arm, 'Come on. Let's go and find ourselves a drink and a little peace and quiet.'

Eve had no idea where he would dig up such a thing as a peaceful corner with all the revelry going around them. Nor was she terribly sure how they both came to be lightheartedly forging their way amidst a press of bodies. Shouldering a path through for her, her tall companion obviously had somewhere in mind. Some minutes later her heart stopped beating for a moment as they trod the banana path—the very same which earlier in the afternoon she had fled from. Now the leaves of the fruit palms were black silhouettes against the electric blue starlit sky, and the route, hitherto unknown to her, unfolded between great rocks draped with wild blossom which exuded a powerful night scent.

His hand on her elbow the man she had spent so many anguished hours thinking about, guided her expertly through the shadows. But now she was too lightheaded to recall her misery at Rex's proposed plan for her. She was filled with a kind of careless abandon and she felt that to some extent her mood was shared by the figure beside her.

They came out onto a tranquil beach bathed in moonlight. Bordering the whispering lap of the waves were the remnants of the afternoon's coconut sherbet and rum potion rivalry. The palm-leaved thatch over the dais where the competitors had been handed their prizes now shaded the moon's rays from the stage instead of the hot sunshine. Columns of unused sampling beakers gleamed white where they leaned against the bole of a tamarind tree, and a discarded necklace of flowers hung, still vivid with life if a little limp, from one of its branches.

In a lamplit glow a beach bar still operated. One or two Creoles who like themselves favoured a quiet spot at the rather late hour, were engaged in desultory conversation. The barman was busy with his cocktail shaker. It was a typical West Indian scene Eve thought, with the palms, the silvery ocean, the rustic bar and its beaming ebony-skinned attendant.

Rydal Grantham led her to one of the crudely fashioned bar stools and assisted her on to it. Her arms resting on the cool surface of the bar, his big frame draped against it alongside her she felt expansive and even adventurous. 'I'm always hearing about these rum concoctions,' she said daringly. 'I've a good mind to try one.'

'Are you telling me,' one dark eyebrow lifted

disbelievingly, 'that you haven't sampled the island's most renowned product and you've been here all of . . .?'

'Five days,' she supplied with a slight lurch of her heart.

'We must rectify that right away.' Sloping a hard grin he ordered a ti punch for her and one for himself. 'This is no relation to the punch as we know it back home,' he informed her as they watched the barman at work. 'This omnipresent drink is a short snort of rum, sugarcane syrup and a dash of lime.'

The end result wasn't bad Eve decided, sipping experimentally from her glass. The aircraft designer drank like an old hand and an extension of their lighthearted mood in his eyes he queried, 'Where are you from, Miss Bowen?'

'Ingledene in Sussex,' she said simply.

'Sounds like some place well off the beaten track,' he gleamed. 'I've never heard of it.'

'It's a small village sandwiched between Edenbury and Foxhurst on the Uckfield road,' she enlightened him with a twinkling look.

'Now I know why I've never heard of it.' He winced. And taking out cigarettes, 'You're a long way from home. What made you choose Martinique for a holiday?'

'I was told that a helping of Caribbean sunshine would do me the world of good, our winters being what they are—so here I am!'

She didn't want to think about Rex just now. And anyway as far as she was concerned she was and had always been simply a tourist here.

'You packed your bags and took the advice, just like that?'

'Just like that!' Though she seldom indulged in the habit she accepted a cigarette from the case he offered.

'Looks like I'm going to have to amend that

indefatigable tag I gave you to intrepid.' His manner was joking. 'You'd have to be that just to hop a plane and come all this way on your own. Unless of course you're with a package tour?'

'No. I'm not with a package tour,' she said, fingering her cigarette.

He put a flame under it watching as she inhaled then turned his gaze to the view. 'It's a good time to come to Martinique.' He put his gold lighter under his own cigarette and blew the smoke out towards the sea. 'It's the driest and relatively coolest period. I usually try and get out here around this time myself, although my stay on this occasion is likely to be considerably more prolonged.'

She sensed a temporary steeling over of his mood and a little breathlessly made no comment. Devoting herself entirely to her ti punch she saw thankfully that he was content to do the same and for a while they gave themselves to the mellow atmosphere at the bar.

In thought however Eve was not idle. She knew so much about this man who in every other sense was a stranger to her. She wondered if he missed the sophisticated life he was used to as a sought-after craftsman in aeronautics, and found it a little incredible that he had achieved the kind of fame Rex had spoken of, so early in his career. In years she wouldn't have put him at more than thirty-eight or thirty-nine. She also thought of the women he was accustomed to mixing with, fashionably clothed most likely, and expensively coiffured. For a moment she was acutely conscious of her own simple hair-style and her dress in which she had picked successive crops of fruit in the vicarage orchard.

The sound of surf falling on the beach came to her ears. In the distance, beyond the forest growth, the music so typical of these Windward Isles fell like droplets on the warm air. Rydal Grantham must have followed her train of thought then for he broke the silence to comment, 'It's hard to believe that such a variety of notes can be coaxed out of oil drums.'

'Is that all they are?' Eve asked disbelievingly.

'With a few refinements from the old days.' He nodded. 'It started in Trinidad when "the pans" as they are called, were used for the first time in a carnival parade. Since then players have hailed from all walks of life in these islands, most of them seeking a creative outlet from the poverty they were reared in. Nowadays a pan tuner commands a good deal of respect. He tempers the drums with heat, then uses a sledge hammer to make indentations that will produce the best steel band sound when struck with mallets.'

'I like the music.' Eve inclined an ear. 'But I would imagine it could get monotonous after a while.'

'To our ears, yes,' he agreed. 'However they don't all turn out pop and jumbled jazz. Some musicians have repertoires which include Mozart and Bach.'

This brought a smile to Eve's lips and his own stern mouth lapsed crooked. 'I'm beginning to sound like that indulgent guide again,' he said drily. He paused reflectively and to Eve it looked as though the hand on his glass tensed. 'Maybe I should take up showing visitors around the island full time,' he spoke to his drink an odd glint in his eyes. Then turning to her he asked with harsh amusement, 'How do you see me as a benign travel courier, Miss Bowen?'

Eve felt that it was a loaded question especially as she was not supposed to know about the business from which it stemmed. Heart thudding she smiled it away by openly glancing at her watch and stating, 'I really ought to be thinking of getting back to Fort-de-France. It's almost eleven forty-five, and if as you say there's a bus at midnight . . .'

'You wouldn't get on it.' He placed his glass down. 'It will be bursting at the seams with aunts, cousins, children and gifts for the city stew pots. But don't worry I can make a detour on my way home.'

Eve froze at his words. 'I'd really rather . . .'

'Consider it part of the guided tour service.' He placed a hand on her arm. 'Just give me the name of your hotel and I'll drop you off on the drive through town.'

Making their way back along the deserted banana path, Eve was tempted, not for the first time that evening, to run from him. But once in his car at the edge of the village she saw the idiocy of such a move. She couldn't remain in Corobrier all night, and there was nothing to stop her leaving the car the moment they reached Fort-de-France.

Asking to be set down just anywhere in town however proved more difficult than she had imagined. Rydal Grantham had his own views on the matter. 'The discotheques around here are very local and very crowded,' he said crisply. 'With no tourists about at this late hour it would be better, I think, if I took you straight to your hotel.'

Once again Eve was trapped. Short of bolting from the moving car there was nothing she could do. 'Do you know the Pension Desirade?' she asked in a pale, but steady voice.

'I don't know it, but I can find it,' he said, picking up speed. 'What avenue is it on?'

'It's along the Rue Dupius,' she replied, aware that he had not expected to have to go deeper into the old part of the town.

He made no comment but followed her hazy instructions through the dimly-lit narrow streets. Her pent-up breath escaped gradually through stiff lips when she saw at last the familiar, tiny forecourt ahead with its cascading bougainvillaea illuminated by the lights of the interior. It may be a cheap *pension* but it was all she would have been able to afford if she had

truly made this trip on her own. And at the moment it
was a haven she couldn't wait to retire to.

The man who had insisted on driving her all the way
pulled up alongside the unprepossessing entrance. He
reached across her to open the door but Eve had
already fumbled for the handle in her desire to cut short
his stay. 'Thank you for the lift back to town, Mr
Grantham,' she said, stepping out. 'And also for the
conducted tour of Corobrier. Goodbye.'

'Goodbye, Miss Bowen.' He leaned across to take the
door before she could close it. 'And don't forget, stick
with the other tourists from now on. You're less likely
to get yourself into a fix that way.'

'I'll do that,' she replied briefly, moving off. He
waited until she had entered the *pension* then clicked
the door to and sped away.

Upstairs in her room Eve fell thankfully against the
locked door, feeling as though she had just come
through a raging gale. But exhausted as she was, both
physically and mentally, she couldn't relax or simply go
to bed. She moved around her confined quarters as
though the haven had now become a cage and sought
air in the end out on the tiny balcony overlooking
corrugated tin roof-tops and the straggle of alley-way
greenery bathed in shadow. There was no sign of the
receding car of course. Rydal Grantham would by this
time be well on his way to his house on the Atlantic side
of the island.

She looked up at the stars thankful that it was over.
She had met Rex's aircraft designer by a wicked fluke
of fate, but it wouldn't happen again. Nothing would
induce her to succumb to her brother's pleading a
second time. Nobody knew better than her that her
goodbye to the big Englishman tonight had been final.
And yet . . . her slender hands gripped the iron rail until
the knuckles showed white as she viewed the heavens
. . . he wasn't that easy to dispel from her mind—or her

heart. She knew she was attracted to him. She had known it from the first moment when he had transported her in his arms to his beach bungalow after she had collapsed on the sand. His very touch had awoken in her the realisation that she was a woman. And caught tightly against him, as she had been, when she had crashed into him while trying to escape to the bus this afternoon was, no matter how much she tried to deny it to herself both then and now, a palpitatingly agreeable sensation.

And every incident of her—on the face of it—casual evening with him was engraved on her mind. She could recall, not unpleasantly, his every gesture, his varying expressions, always inured but sometimes laced with whimsey. His hard-bitten smile and the way he relaxed his big frame whenever his humour equally of the flinty brand became prolonged. It was as well, she threw her gaze a little distractedly around, that one week of her three week holiday was almost at an end. Though she wouldn't see Rydal Grantham again she would know no peace until she had left Martinique. How could she when every fibre of her being was tuned to his presence here on the island?

CHAPTER FIVE

Eve had no appetite for breakfast the next morning. The tray which had been sent up to her room remained where it had been placed outside her door. After gazing unseeingly at the activity in the street below her balcony she decided that a cup of coffee, after all, might ease her throbbing temples. She hadn't had too good a night.

She was halfway to the door when it opened and the tray was brought in by Rex. He was aglow with the new day and looked lean and handsome in lemon beach shirt and white jeans. 'Great, Eve! Great!' He waltzed to the table, setting the tray down and eyeing it with mild disdain. 'There ought to be something special here like champagne on a day like this. Champers for breakfast, no less!'

Eve blinked. 'What,' she asked, not sharing his exhilaration for the morning, 'are we celebrating?'

'Your success with Grantham last night, of course. It couldn't have gone better.'

She was glad to be able to have the coffee pot to clutch hold of. Even then her hand trembled slightly as she poured. How could Rex know what had happened last night? The question flashed through her mind. He wasn't there. But he had been informed obviously. By whom? She had to remember that he was a journalist and he was skilled in the art of finding out. Had there been someone in his employ, one of the revellers ostensibly joining in the fun but all the while keeping an eye on her 'progress' with Rydal Grantham? Clearly the watcher had assumed, seeing them both in the thick of the festivities, that all was going according to plan and had reported as such.

'Keep up the good work.' Her brother was beaming, but he appeared edgy. 'I only came to say that I'm disappearing from the scene for a while.'

She realised then that he had no intention of prolonging his stay. 'Disappearing?' she echoed in a dazed way.

'It wouldn't do now for you and me to be seen together.' He grinned. 'The whole thing will be blown sky-high if anybody gets wind that I'm around.'

'The whole thing?' she queried a little coldly. 'What thing? I met your aircraft designer at Corobrier true, but we were ... well just ships that pass in the night if you like. I'm afraid you're banking far too much on——'

'Leave me to know my business, sweetheart,' came the drawling reply. 'Grantham will be back. He needs a friend like you. Maybe you don't know it but you're a pretty soothing person to be with, Eve. There's a smiling peace in your eyes.'

'But your room at the hotel ...?' She closed her ears frantically to this kind of talk. She didn't want to be anything in Rydal Grantham's life. Not the way Rex organised things.

'I've never had a room here,' her brother disclosed breezily. 'I booked you in at the desk on our arrival. My digs, however, are some distance from here.'

Coming on top of her already shocked senses this new revelation robbed Eve of all coherent thinking. She could only say numbly, 'But you always told me you were on the floor below in ...'

'Room number twenty-five,' he filled in for her, nodding. 'That was just so you wouldn't feel nervous about being here on your own. I knew that I'd be a fool to let myself be linked with you in any way. Grantham himself might not worry about you now, but you can bet your life his henchmen will have you checked out.' With a finger he tapped his temple smilingly. 'Just a little thinking ahead, Sis. Now all they'll find is that you are staying here alone. And if a handsome young man,' he paused to twinkle vainly, has been seen to drift in and out of your life lately then that should only serve to stimulate Grantham's interest, so to speak.'

'Sometimes, Rex,' she placed the coffee pot down squarely, 'I could cheerfully disown you as a brother.'

'That's okay, so long as you don't disown this thing we've set up together.' There was something metallic in his humour.

'Together!' Her own tones were brittle. 'After you got me out here on false——'

'Look, I have to go.' There was a flicker of impatience in his manner. 'I'll keep in touch, don't worry.'

Still benumbed she watched him make for the door, finding her tongue at the last moment to protest. 'But, Rex! You're not just going to leave me like this, all alone in this place . . .'

'If things go as planned,' he winked, 'you won't be alone for long.' He turned in the doorway, eyed her and advised, 'Have some coffee!' Then in his jaunty way he was gone.

As it turned out Eve wasn't far behind him. After her brother had left she was convinced with agitation that he might possibly be right. Supposing the aircraft designer did pass by the *pension*? There was no reason to think that he would ever give her another thought but, remote as the chances were, she couldn't risk meeting up with him again.

So she hurriedly dressed and left the Desirade; left the only place in town where she could be traced to. She would not return until the dark hours. Though heaven knew how she was going to spend the day. She had no money except a little loose change in her purse. Following the pursuits of a tourist in Fort-de-France was a costly business. She would have to go everywhere on foot. But at least there was always the park.

La Savane was near the water's edge in the heart of the city. Here there were flowers, fountains, promenades and playgrounds. Eve admired Bengal roses, royal palms, travellers palms and giant bamboo until lunch-time. At one of the side-walk cafes on the harbour front she bought a roll and mineral water and afterwards directed her steps towards the *Musée Départementale* where she spent the afternoon browsing among slave-irons, skeletal bones, island costumes and old French maps.

Night, she was learning, dropped suddenly in these Windward Isles, around six o'clock, but she killed time until eight before she felt it was safe to return to the Pension Desirade. All was silent in the little foyer when she arrived, as it mostly was with few foreign guests in this part of the town. She went up in the cage-lift on tenterhooks, but began to relax when no one had stopped her with messages and there was no sign of there having been any callers when she entered her room.

Footsore and weary she showered and changed and went down for a meal. Afterwards she fell into bed cursing Rex for his callousness and rigid adherence to a wild idea. He didn't know it, or he refused to believe it, but she had long since opted out of his schemes.

Every morning she set out after breakfast and every evening she returned shattered after several hours on foot ostensibly sightseeing. On the fourth morning she began to wonder if after all she was letting her nerves get the better of her. In three days nothing unusual had happened at the *pension*. No one had called, and there had been no messages. Rex may be a very wily journalist, but he couldn't expect to know the working of men's minds. Certainly not a man like Rydal Grantham. If he was basing all his hopes on the aircraft designer's reacting in the usual way to his staged events, then perhaps she had no further need to worry.

She dragged her steps, however, towards the market where a high roof arched over an entire city block. Here when one's eyes grew accustomed to the dim light of the interior, there were pyramids of green breadfruit to be seen, as well as velvety brown sapodillas, pineapples, guavas, pails of tawny tiger lilies and pastel gerbera daisies—all lying on long trestle tables. Around a centre pillar piles of straw baskets and hats leaned precariously, and jamming the narrow aisles the Martiniquais, who seldom meet, be it four times a day, with less than a handshake and usually an embrace, caused more commotion than the roosters crowing defiantly over the hurly-burly.

The market was an old haunt for Eve, but it was good for whiling away the morning. In the afternoon she could visit yet another free museum. It was seven-thirty when she finally wended her way back along the side-streets to the Pension Desirade. Bone-weary and flat-spirited, on one thing she was decided. No more tramping around Fort-de-France. Quite clearly nothing was going to happen. She had got the jitters because of Rex's optimistic outlook on everything. But really if she'd thought about it there was no earthly reason why Rydal Grantham should look her up again. Socially they were planets apart. He belonged to the sophisti-cated world of successful professional people, and she was a village mouse, at present giving the appearance of scratching out a holiday on Martinique.

And what else was there? They had met by accident on a couple of occasions. Two separate incidents which he had probably forgotten and which she was doing her best to push to the back of her mind. No. She wouldn't run anymore. She was through with dodging shadows conjured up by her brother's colourful imagination. For instance she was going to go back to the *pension* tonight and have a delicious, lingering warm soak. Later she would dine leisurely in the basement *salle à manger*, and instead of going to bed when she returned to her room she intended to put her feet up in the most comfortable armchair and lose herself in an epic second-hand novel she had unearthed at an oddments booth on the way home. Tomorrow she would think of some other way to pamper herself around the *pension*. Her room and board were paid for at least. And Rex could come back when he liked. She would enjoy her holiday somehow.

She turned the last corner and saw her lodging-house half-way along the narrow street. It was aglow and homely-looking despite its being wedged between shanty dwellings and small-time tin-roofed businesses. But under a deep blue sky lit by constant golden sunshine, nothing in Martinique looked shabby. And at night-time, as now, the brilliant stars above and the fireflies dancing in the wayside greenery gave even the most haphazard hut a romantic appearance.

With visions of propping up her aching feet she stepped it out over the last few yards. Not with any sense of hurry so much as pleasurable anticipation—until she felt another presence in the alley, behind her.

The sleek dark car had turned the corner when she had. Now she was aware of it sliding quietly alongside her. The lights of the *pension* spilled over on to the minute forecourt. She supposed that the driver had lost his way and was hoping for some enlightenment. Just the same—she had almost reached the illuminated space when a familiar voice spoke from the car window. 'Miss Bowen? Good evening. I hope I didn't give you a scare?'

Eve stood stock still in the shadows. She turned. Her face may have paled, but no, it wasn't with fright. It was an overwhelming, an overall sweet pain which had weakened her. She hadn't realised how much she had wanted to hear that voice again. 'Good evening, Mister Grantham.' She sounded shaky and covered up with, 'I *was* a little startled . . .' In her confusion she could get no further with manufacturing excuses. She had prayed all along that she would never see him again, yet somewhere inside her these past days had been the bleak hope that he would reappear.

'My apologies,' he was saying deeply. 'I've been cruising around the district waiting for you to arrive. They told me at the *pension* this afternoon that you usually return about eight.'

So she had trapped herself simply by routine, even though she had gone far afield to avoid him.

'Yes, I usually get back from my sightseeing trips about this time.' She forced a note of lightness into her trembling voice.

'That's what I've come to see you about,' he said, unfolding his big shape from the car and taking her elbow in its familiar grasp. 'Can we sit and have a drink?'

'If you like.' To her ears her words sounded high-pitched and she wished she didn't have to keep making fatuous replies. Her pulses raced and a choir sang in her heart at his touch. All this because he had turned up again! What was she going to do with herself!

He led her to a forecourt table where Bayfor, an all-duties youth at the *pension*, came to see what the bizarre foreign couple wanted at this hour of the evening. There were no views here, nothing to attract tourists in this tucked-away part of the town. Still, the European pair seemed content enough with their ti punches and each other. Eve could read the boy's thoughts and she strove to shatter the illusion by saying loudly in his presence, 'I can only stay a little while, I'm . . . going to be rather busy later on.'

'You're not planning to go to one of those cheap night shows are you?' The big man spoke with asperity when the boy had gone. 'They're no place for a woman on her own. If you've let someone push a ticket on to you . . .'

'No, I . . .' Alarmed Eve saw how one small untruth could enmesh her. Thankfully the way was not left for her to concoct more fairy tales for she heard him saying over his drink, 'I've been thinking about you on your own on the island. You're probably doing and seeing all the wrong things. For instance I bet you've been foot-slogging round the museums and studying the city landmarks, right?'

'Well . . . yes.' Feeling her colour rise, oddly enough this was one aspect she didn't have to lie about.

'You're not really seeing Martinique.' He shook his head. 'That stuff's all right for the package-tour types, but there is another side to the island.' And after a pause, 'I'm going into the mountains tomorrow afternoon to see some friends of mine. Planter Ignace Guamel and his family grow sugar and bananas. It occurred to me,' he said almost casually, 'that you might find it an interesting trip.'

Would she! But before she could begin to glow at the idea Eve shrugged and tried to sound offhand. 'You forget I tried a little island trekking on my own before I took to viewing city sights.'

'And got yourself into tricky situations on the occasions I was around,' he said drily. 'This time you won't be steering in the wrong direction. I'll be at the wheel. Incidentally what happened to your car?'

The question, though lazily put, caught her off-guard. He had seen her returning on foot now, and he knew that she had reached Corobrier by bus. 'I . . . it was too expensive to hire for more than a few days . . .' she came out with at last. Rex had driven that first day when the car had been waiting for her round the headland of the beach, but since then he had taken over the rented vehicle for his own use. In any case she had never professed to be loaded with francs for her holiday on the island.

Nodding as though her reply was unimportant the

aircraft expert said, 'How does two o'clock tomorrow afternoon suit you?'

So he was intent on making the date stick. What could she do? Well . . . she toyed with her glass, she had been on the point of giving herself completely to this holiday. She had resolved to forget Rex and his dubious schemes. So why not forget him far away from the *pension*? The hinterland of the island was what interested her most and if her senses were a little intoxicated because it happened to be this man who had suggested the outing surely that was nobody's business but her own.

'All right,' she said, hardly caring now that there was an eager note in her voice. 'I'll wait for you here on the forecourt if you like.'

'Fine.' He rose, leaving his drink half-finished. 'I won't keep you. You must be tired after your day out.'

'I am rather.' She smiled gratefully. 'I was just planning a warm soak to get rid of the city dust.'

'Is that what was going to keep you busy for the rest of the evening?' A roguish glint replaced the flint in his eyes.

'I've just acquired a good book' she confessed with a merry light. 'I couldn't wait to read it.'

'If everything winds up neatly at the end,' he said with a change in his humour, 'don't believe it. Life has a way of not working out pat somehow.'

In the space of the second that it took Eve to lower her lashes he had recovered his suave mood. 'Two tomorrow and bring a light wrap. It drops a little cooler in the mountains towards evening.'

She didn't wait until he reached his car but turned and made her way through a radiant blur indoors. She didn't read her book that night and her bath though laced with a double helping of perfumed salts, was taken in an abstract way. All her instincts told her that it was wrong to give in to the wishes of her heart. She should pack at once; leave the *pension*, leave the town, leave the island! If only she could find the will and the strength to put such a plan into practice.

CHAPTER SIX

THEY took the west coast road north from Fort-de-France the next afternoon, leapfrogging from hill to hill. Steep ridges stretched from the Carbet peaks towards the centre of the island, to drop abruptly into the Caribbean. Between these promontories, wherever the sea washed a beach of glistening black sand, fishing villages nestled. Eve viewed everything with silent rapture. Rex had said that Martinique was very French and it was out here in the countryside where one noticed it most. In the warm sun men and boys in woollen berets cycled by, and in some of the more populated communities restaurant proprietors were putting out tables and chairs to form pavement cafés for the afternoon.

Cruising through the virgin greenery of the foothills the man beside her fulfilled his chosen role as guide by explaining to her something about their surroundings. Apparently rain-bearing trade winds, robbed of their moisture by the high central range gave little sustenance to these parched leeward slopes during the dry season. Yet fields of sugar-cane were able to find toe-holds in the upper reaches of some valleys or fonds as they were called. Occasionally fragant odours drifted down to them from a grey stone sugar-mill at the head of a valley.

The Guamels' plantation, Lazeret, was in one of these rifts, the sugar-cane growing six foot high or more alongside the criss-crossing tracks. In the car they passed barefooted cutters hacking away with gleaming machetes. Their black faces glistening with sweat they grinned good-naturedly at Eve. Women in rough cotton overalls balanced bundles of grass-tied cane on their gay turbanned heads, some munching sticks of the sweet growth as they moved in their graceful way towards the bullock carts.

Slim, stoop-shouldered Ignace Guamel admitted freely that they were short on mechanisation around the place. On a terrace in front of the house shaded by huge mango trees he told Eve, with Rydal Grantham acting as interpreter as she spoke no French, that some time they might get round to modernising the plantation, but no one was in any particular hurry. Judging by the twinkle in his faded blue eyes he preferred things as they were, and sensing the lazy air of contentment everywhere Eve was just as twinklingly inclined to agree with him.

After refreshments he took them on a bumpy tour of his sugar-cane fields. 'Couldn't do without this runabout.' He patted his ancient vehicle proudly. And waving an arm to where mile upon mile of cane stretched, on the point of turning from green to gold under the cloud-flecked blue sky, 'All this land belongs to my family.' The proud light reappeared in his old eyes as he added, 'I have twelve children and thirty-eight grandchildren.'

They must all be in the fields, or almost all. Later, in a garden ablaze with bougainvillaea, overlooking the sea and the blurred shape of Dominica, next in the island chain, Eve met Ignace's wife. Monique was a small woman with white wavy hair and young-looking weathered features. Four-years-old Louis Emile, a grandson of the family was sailing his toy boat in a makeshift bathing pool.

'The pool is fed from a mountain stream,' Ignace explained. Eve saw where the stream emerged from the pool to turn a small turbine. From there it tumbled on to the distillery, revolving huge rollers. After this feat, she was shown how it plunged over a cliff to the beach more than two hundred feet below. In the distillery, or *rhummerie* as it was called in the local patois, she watched massive rollers squeezing juice from sugar-cane to make rum, just about as it did when the walls were built in the early eighteen hundreds.

The aircraft specialist translated most of Ignace's chat though sometimes Eve suspected he left out the more colourful bits. When the two of them were sharing a grin in the distillery she asked, 'What was that he said?' feeling she was being deprived of a joke.

'The old timer was just telling me he has trouble coaxing the male members of his clan into this side of the business,' the big man enlightened her. 'They have a saying on the island, "Boys make rum; men make sugar".' His grin broadening as he moved on and watching him, wide-shouldered, indomitable, Eve was in no doubt what category he would have fallen into had he been a plantation owner.

Gazing down to where the village of Marimant leaned against the cliff base, Ignace eyed the position of the sun and told them, 'It's almost time for the fishing fleet to come in. There's a path down from here if you'd like to take a look at Marimant.'

While work continued on the sugar plantation Eve and Rydal Grantham followed the route round the hillside to the sandy cleft below. When they arrived the fishing boats had landed on the black, scaly beach. Crewmen were striding to the weighing scales with their catch. Eve stood back as four-foot dolphins tipped the scales at thirty-six pounds. Pointed out for her also were smaller kingfish, redfish and ten-inch flying fish netted, she learned, as they spawned among dried banana leaves scattered on the water's surface.

'Ignace reckons they're the finest boatmen on the island,' the big man told her. 'He wants us to stay the night and come down at dawn tomorrow when they're setting off.'

'Stay?' Eve carefully eyed the horizon from where they stood against a beach rail.

'Why not?' The voice sounded slightly harsh if humorous. 'You're footloose and fancy-free, aren't you?'

'I suppose I am.' Smiling, she thrust a whisper of uncertainty to the back of her mind.

Retracing their steps up the hillside it was not as easy making the ascent as it had been coming down. Pausing for breath at one point Eve turned to gaze back to where the fishing village nestled against the cliff, bracing itself against stiff winds and pounding surf. Her flower-sprigged dress fluttered in the breeze as did her companion's thin shirt and casual slacks.

'Rest here for a while.' The aviation man drew her into a sheltered hollow where a sawn off log offered a seat for one. 'With the cutting season upon the Guamels there'll be nothing doing at the house for another half hour or so.'

She sat but demurred at the cigarettes he offered. When he had lit one up for himself and was draped comfortably against a locust tree he asked, 'Reckon your tour of Lazeret has improved your knowledge on how the other half lives, here on Martinique?'

'Considerably,' she admitted. 'Although it depends what you mean by "the other half". The Pension Desirade is not exactly situated in the Nob Hill section of town.' Her reply was made not with any feeling of embarrassment but more with amusement.

'That's right.' His own whimsical expression showed that he had caught her meaning. 'You're quite a way from the luxury hotel strata in your Dupius street. But I take it you're okay at the Desirade?'

She nodded still lighthearted. 'It's quiet, clean—and cheap.'

He blew out his cigarrette smoke idly. His keen blue eyes on her, he asked with a curious grin, 'What made you come out here on a shoe-string?'

She shrugged. 'Desperation, I suppose. I thought I was content enough in Ingledene until I had it pointed out to me that there were other places less foggy and less rainy than Novemberish England.'

'And what do you do in this village of yours—Ingledene?'

She smiled reflectively at his lazy question. 'I thrust newspapers into the hands of dashing commuters for the London train, and I serve tobacco to the local pensioners on pay day.'

'You're a business woman?'

'Hardly. Major Llewellyn owns the shop on the high street where I work.'

'And I expect you've got some hollyhock cottage you go home to every night.' He viewed her drily.

'No again,' she said with humour. 'I live in three rooms over the local bakery.'

'Alone?' He altered his stance slightly.

'Not quite.' There was laughter in her eyes. 'I share the place with the mice from below. If you've ever lived over a bakery you'll know what I mean.'

'No, I've never lived over a bakery, Miss Bowen.' The lightness of the moment seemed temporarily lost as he turned to cast his glance over the sea and tacked on a little tightly, 'But sometimes I wish I had.' After a pause he was back against the tree to state laconically, 'You must be finding all this quite a jump from the life you've known back home?'

'Oh, I don't know!' Eve couldn't find it in her heart to be serious. 'As niece of the Ingledene vicar, now deceased, I do have a certain standing among the villagers.'

'Vicar's niece, eh?' The glinting blue eyes narrowed. 'I'll have to watch my language.'

'Don't feel inhibited on my account,' she said lightly. 'I've heard it all when shins are barked and no one has the right change on the early morning dash for the station. It might be away from the madding crowds where I am, but it's hardly a sheltered life.'

'Nevertheless I envy you, Eve Bowen.'

She found herself a little startled at his forthright comment and his introspective, bitter smile. Taking a breath she ventured, 'I can't imagine a man like you being content with the inertia of village life.'

'Can't you?' There was irony in his expression. 'The island of Martinique is ninety per cent inertia but I don't think I stand out like a sore finger, do I?'

Eve hesitated at his remark. To her he was a man whose phlegmatic masculinity would make him the focal point of attention in any gathering, but she caught his meaning. 'No, you don't appear out of place here,' she agreed. 'But then I believe you pointed out, your stay on the island is only temporary.'

'As temporary as I want to make it.' His reply was crisp. 'Which can mean two months or twenty years.'

'Maybe *I* should envy *you*.' She strove to keep the mood frivolous. 'My own stay on the island is limited to two more weeks. I'm already starting the second of my three weeks holiday.'

'And then it's back to thatched cottages and rural life in the rain.' His humour was a little brackish. He seemed dissatisfied with his smoke and dropping the half cigarette on the ground tamped out the glow with the sole of his shoe. 'My background is considerably more sheet glass and metal fixtures.' He lifted his dark head, his mouth wry. 'I live atop an office block in the centre of commercial London. It's befitting my position.' He spoke with a kind of self-mockery. 'And do you know what my position is?'

'You buy and sell islands.' Eve was deliberately facetious in the hope that the subject might be changed. But Rydal Grantham appeared keen, in a tautly smiling way, to go on. 'I design aeroplanes,' he said with pseudo pride. 'I dream up the shape of the fuselage—

the body to you—and the wings; not just to look pretty but to control the airflow for safety and speed.'

'It must be exciting work,' Eve commented quietly.

'It's a job.' There was a touch of satire about his grin. 'I'm the big boss, you see. An aircraft is so complex I have many sub-designers working under me. They submit their plans for—well shall we say, the oxygen system, the electronics system, the girders, the undercarriage, radar—all of which I coordinate in my design.'

'And aren't you happy in your profession?' It was an unavoidable question brought on by his corrosive, self-effacing humour. But Eve asked it for another reason.

All afternoon she had moved beside this man with a song in her heart. She had viewed the plantation, listened to the chat, and been impressed by all he had pointed out to her, but it had been enough just to feel his nearness, just to muse over the deep timbre of his voice, to suppress an agreeable tremor every time his fingers rested on her arm to move on. Now, watching his set jaw, divining a smouldering dissatisfaction in him beneath his steely banter, she was filled with a compassion, the force of which overwhelmed her. More than anything she wanted to know what troubled him. She wanted to know why there was sometimes a look of angry disillusionment in his eyes; the reason for the occasional sad tilt to his case-hardened smile. She wanted to know because her heart was touched by all she saw in him.

'What is happiness in your work?' he was asking cynically. 'A big salary, friends in the right places, or someone you can trust?'

'I'm hardly qualified to offer an opinion.' She lowered her lashes. 'But if every one has to answer to you then it's within your power to arrange things to suit yourself?'

'Ah but there are snags.' His grin was warped. 'The building of aeroplanes needs a constant transfusion of money and the backers sometimes have their own ideas on policy. They frequently gather round a polished table to ask for a progress report on the current stage of development, but you can never tell what else will crop up.'

'I gather you don't like these board meetings?' Eve murmured shrewdly.

He shot her a glance, swung it away to the sea and said almost to himself with a grim smile, 'The last one I attended was a dilly.'

Viewing his well-shaped head Eve was lost for a foothold to continue. She said softly and somewhat helplessly, 'You're a long way from your work here on Martinique.'

'I am and I aren't,' he drawled paradoxically. 'Mine is the kind of vocation that seems to follow me around.'

'Are you trying to escape from it?' She hugged her bare arms as the sun sank behind the cliff.

'No. But I'm here to make a decision. It's a weighty one but it can wait.' He turned. 'You're feeling the cold. Let's get back to the plantation.'

At dusk members of the Guamel family converged on the sprawling old house overlooking the Caribbean. After twenty introductions Eve lost count of numbers and names. On a patio screened by cinnamon shrubs, steaming bowls of food were passed from one end of the phenomenally long table to the other, and afterwards two sons of the family began strumming catchy calypso tunes on their guitars. There may have been toddlers crooning to themselves on the lawn and couples engrossed in undercover tiffs and chat but Eve found it an immensely peaceful scene. The canopy of blue-black sky sprinkled with stars, the oyster-silk sheen of the ocean, and a breeze scented and warmly benign now, stirring the leaves of the mango trees.

A peaceful scene—her glance shifted and inadvertently came up against that of her companion on the trip where he idly pulled on a cigarette beside the calypso players—shared with a man who was not at peace.

CHAPTER SEVEN

SHE slept in a huge old-fashioned four poster bed shrouded by a gauzy mosquito net. There was no mistaking that she was in a French household when she tasted the delicious crusty bread warm from the oven the next morning. With coffee and home-made fruit marmalade she felt as though she had partaken of a banquet and was more than ready to accompany the aviation man back to the beach at Marimant.

Golden shafts of sunlight slanted over the cliffs as they went down hand in hand. This appeared a more practical way to make the steep descent, but even if her sandals had been sturdy enough to stand up to the sometimes treacherous scree she would not have complained at the strong grasp which enclosed her fingers.

There were forty fishing boats or more preparing for the launching. Three men crews were poised beside their rough carved crafts, the helmsmen of each carefully weighing up the rhythm of the cresting swell. When it was deemed fit to go the crews leapt in, the two bow men rowing frantically. In a matter of seconds the prows of the launched boats would shoot skywards. Eve held her breath. The flimsy fishing craft seemed certain to snap in two atop the swirling wave, but a few more seconds and they were in calmer waters. Here, stowing the oars, the men rigged a short mast with a sail braced by a supple bamboo pole.

A more picturesque sight than forty odd sampan-like sails gliding forth into the flush of early morning could not have been imagined, and Eve stood enthralled until each sail had become a speck against the horizon. Then turning his glance the man beside her said in amused tones, 'I think we are now about to witness a less professional display.'

Eve soon saw what he meant for the youngsters of the community had begun proudly launching their own boats. They were mere logs but they had been gaily painted and sturdy young bodies rode astride them through the barrier of foam, later turning and careening shorewards, their logs riding the breakers like surfboards. All had names and Eve caught sight of one.

'L'hirondelle du été,' she spelled out.

'Summer swallow,' her broad-shouldered companion translated, watching a wisp of hair at her temples as it was tugged by the breeze.

It was after twelve when they finally left Lazaret for the ride back to Fort-de-France. Once in the city there was no need, this time, to direct the way to her holiday digs. They pulled up outside the Pension Desirade and she was preparing to alight when her travel host stayed her hand on the door by reaching across with his own to say, 'Are you game for another guided tour this afternoon?'

'But we've only just arrived back from one.' Her heart missed a beat.

'I know. But we've got time for a quick lunch and a change of clothes and I could meet you back here at two.'

'Where would we go?' Happiness coursed along her veins.

'Well . . .' He drummed his fingers on the dashboard. 'I could show you the rain forest—an enchanted world of ferns.'

'All right.' If he had suggested a trip to a barren wasteland she would have said yes. 'I'll be ready at two.'

So began Eve's grand tour of Martinique. She saw the giant ferns north of the island, and the petrified savanna forest in the south. She watched the harvesting of bananas and pineapples on coastal plantations—her fellow countryman had friends everywhere—and wandered through the ubiquitous sugar fields and valleys dotted with the old stone mills. She grew to love these dim, high-roofed buildings redolent with the tempting aroma of cane juice simmering in huge vats. More than once they quenched their thirst on these outings with freshly squeezed cane juice which, to her mind, had a grassy flavour.

A week flew by. They were days which ran into each other, separated only by the varying degrees of joy. There were, however, two things which, looking back, stood out in Eve's mind. She had seen the men who guarded the aircraft expert's privacy several times. The neat-suited pair of Martiniquais were always in the background somewhere, either following along by car or prudently mingling among family members on a plantation visit. Even on that first afternoon at Lazaret she had been aware of their presence at a discreet distance. The other unforgettable happening was an incident which lingered pulsatingly in Eve's consciousness.

She had been watching work at a farm packing shed one afternoon. Barefooted women padded and wrapped the stems of bananas ready for their voyage in refrigerated ships. Eve was intrigued at the speed with which the nimble brown fingers completed the task. She had stepped forward to take a closer look when a sharp gasp from the big man beside her riveted her. In the next split-second he had tugged her swiftly against him and she was staring down at a bristly crawling object which her bare arm had brushed from the bench as she turned.

'Matoutou falaise!' shrieked the nearest woman then promptly stamped a calloused heel on the scurrying shape.

'The local name for a poisonous spider occasionally brought in on bananas,' Rydal Grantham explained.

Eve shuddered against him, turning pale, but the horror quickly passed and was soon forgotten. What did not disappear was the sweet ache of being held close in an embrace which should have been temporary but wasn't. She couldn't have said which one of them was the prime force in prolonging it. She only knew that she had no inclination to withdraw. But withdraw she did when the keen, deep-set blue gaze began exploring hers.

At the end of the week they spent the day at the country home of a Martinique businessman friend of her island guide, where with other guests they boarded two sailing canoes for a swim among the offshore islands. It was a memorable occasion for Eve in more ways than one, but there was a shock waiting for her when she got back to her room at the *pension* at the end of the day.

Rex was lounging in one of the armchairs. 'Eve!' He appeared mildly irritated. 'You've been so damn good at your assignment I've had a job getting hold of you.'

Eve froze when she saw him but she spoke pleasantly enough. 'I'm sorry I've been out a lot, Rex.' She dropped her handbag on a chair. 'I never knew this sugar island in the Caribbean could be so fascinating.'

'Well I'm glad you're finding the work agreeable.' He rose, brightening. 'What I want to know is what headway you've made with Grantham?'

'I ...' she fingered the wrap she had removed from her shoulders '... he's proving a useful guide around Martinique.'

'Yes I know, that's the cover-up.' Rex nodded impatiently. 'But what have you found out so far?'

'Not much,' Eve's throat tightened. 'He's ... not a great talker. Nor am I.'

'But he must have said *something* about his work?'

She forced a shrug and answered the pettish tones

while striving to keep her hands from fidgeting. 'He's mainly concerned with giving me an insight into the local way of life.'

Rex began to pace. 'You realise we've only got one week left,' he said flatly. And giving her a cold direct look. 'So something had better break soon.'

She began moving her things. 'I'm very tired, Rex——'

'You're tired!' He swung on her. 'Listen, Eve, I've sweat blood setting up this scoop. And I don't intend to let it slip through my fingers because of your watery enthusiasm for the job.'

'The only way to stimulate my enthusiasm is to tell me that we're leaving the island right now,' Eve said, white-faced. Inside, her heart was wrung with her words. Could she cut out of her life and her being all thoughts of the man who had been at her side these past days? Forego her last precious week in his company here on Martinique? Yes! She wept a little inwardly. Anything to stop her brother battening on to him.

The strained silence in the room was broken by Rex's quick step forward. 'Listen, Sis.' His smile a little uneasy, he spoke soothingly. 'Just carry on as you are. There's no need to get upset. A lot can happen in a week. It's my guess that Grantham is warming up to coming out with what's biting him. After that you can go back to Ingledene and forget that I ever disrupted your life.'

More likely it would be the other way round. Rex would forget her completely once he was back in his own environment scaling the rungs to success.

He made his way to the door. 'I'll leave you to get some sleep. We can talk again later. Good night, Eve.'

'Good night, Rex,' she said wearily, her back to him as he went out.

They had planned a trip to Diamant, a town to the south of the island. Driving along the next morning the big man eyed her keenly. 'Bad night?'

'No, just a slight headache.' She smiled. 'The breeze will blow it away.'

'If you'd rather not travel . . .'

'Of course! I'm fine.' She brushed aside his concern hoping that the effects of her unpleasant wrangle with Rex would soon cease to be noticeable. Cruising through exotic scenery, the wide-shouldered presence at her side it wasn't difficult to forget her brother. And throughout the days that followed she lived in the see-saw world of happiness and bleak realism. Her imminent return to England weighed like a stone on her heart.

One afternoon they visited Pointe Milou, a wild, breathtaking headland from which on a clear day it was possible to count nine islets in the sea. There were strange cactus-like plants growing everywhere. They had prominent red protuberances and her companion told her, 'They're called *Tête à l'anglais*. Supposed to be named after the British Redcoats.'

Eve inhaled the crisp Atlantic air and gazed out towards the pearly horizon. She sensed the masculine figure at her side. 'I can't believe my brief reference to the botanical has triggered off such profound thoughts,' he said deeply.

'I was thinking of Tuesday and my flight back to England.' She brought her glance in. 'I must be about the best briefed tourist ever to visit Martinique, thanks to you.'

It wouldn't have been out of place to make some equally flippant reply, but his teasing look had sobered at her words and eventually it became as far distant as her own. 'Back to the world of reality,' he murmured harshly. 'You to your rustic Sussex habitat and me . . .'

'I seem to recall that you have a choice,' she put in quickly. 'Two months or twenty years, didn't you say?'

'I can take my time about returning.' He nodded. 'But I've got to decide something in reasonably quick time.'

She knew every line of his rough-hewn countenance by now, and touched at the grim disillusionment she saw there as they stood facing the wild expanse of ocean she said softly, 'If it's as unpleasant as all that why make the decision at all?'

'Because I can't go back,' he replied. 'There's one era of my working life that's closed. But professionally I have to go on. My career is designing aircraft.'

'Perhaps I should be thankful for my simple existence above the village bakery.' Eve smiled with a view to lightening the atmosphere. 'The only important decisions I know about are whether to order a dozen or half a dozen eggs with the week-end groceries, and what daily newspapers I'm likely to have left on my hands at the shop if the railway workers on the seven-thirty to the city are out on strike.'

'There are others.' His tight-lipped expression relaxed into a grin. 'For instance I could tell you a little of what's been on my own mind lately.'

Eve's heart lurched down a step. 'I'm not an authority on professional aeronautics,' she joked feebly.

'No, but you're a good listener.' His blue eyes rested on her. 'And if nothing else that makes for easy talking.'

Eve fixed her gaze on a fishing boat riding the waves but beyond that she was helpless.

'Let's call the plane I've been working on XY43,' he began tightly. 'You could say that in all I've put seven years in on this particular design. Then what do I find? At the last board meeting I went to, one of the directors during the technical talks quite casually mentioned that—shall we say B Company had submitted a tender for parts of the XY etc., aircraft. At that I asked who the hell was leaking information. Nobody outside a list of confidential suppliers, who have already signed statements of secrecy, know anything about the aircraft. And B company is not on our list.'

'What does it mean?' Eve asked trying to read the strain in his features.

'It means that seven years of my work is down the drain,' came the flat reply. 'Messed up because someone, a rival firm—or nation—can take advantage of the leak to put a similar plane on the market. Naturally I walked out of the board meeting. Now what I have to decide is whether to stay with those whose trust is suspect, or take my services elsewhere.'

'I see what you mean.' Eve nodded slowly. 'It's a weighty problem.'

'Weighty but not insoluble.' He smiled lopsidedly. 'And it's my headache not yours. In any case I'm already three parts of the way decided what I'm going to do. There's a third alternative,' he looked at her, 'which I've been giving some thought to—but for now let's get back to the car. There's the remains of a Carib Indian settlement I want to show you while we're over on this side of the island.'

Eve went willingly. Time was running out and if nothing else she wanted to count every second of these remaining days with the big, brooding Englishman.

CHAPTER EIGHT

ON Saturday after a visit to the forest Montravail they were cruising back to town. Normally once in the old section Eve would have been set down outside the Pension Desirade and her escort would have driven off once arrangements for the next sightseeing trip had been made. But on this occasion he took his time weaving through the back streets.

'I've planned something a little different for later on,' he said, swinging the wheel. Eve waited and he went on with a crooked grin, 'I'll admit there will be no notable Martinique features in sight. In fact it's likely to be the other way; tourists everywhere and commercialism as thick as you can get it. In other words a hotel over on the Pointe du Bout resort, dinner and a dance. How does the idea appeal?'

'It appeals very much,' she replied simply, while a radiance within her was almost too painful to contain.

'Okay.' He opened the door for her outside the *pension*. 'I'll pick you up at eight.'

Eve moved indoors as though in a dream. With only two days left of her holiday after tonight she was ready to grasp at anything that would provide her with bitter-sweet memories for the rest of her life.

Minutes before the appointed hour she viewed herself in front of the mirror. She had put on a slim-line, ankle-length dress in a silvery material. It had a halter neckline which displayed her bare arms and back. It was the only evening garment she possessed and one that had seen many a simple parsonage occasion over the years, at Ingledene. Her aunt had always liked it but Eve knew it was dated. She gazed critically at her features through the glass. Nothing outstanding there either. Straight, slim nose, neat mouth, a transparency around the temples. Rex had said there was a smiling peace in her eyes, but she dare not examine too closely the grey-green orbs staring back at her in case she saw something distinctly unpeaceful there; a light that registered the happy turmoil in her heart.

The dress had a matching silver stole which she collected on her way out. The car and Rydal Grantham were waiting for her when she got downstairs and out to the kerb. 'Good. You've brought a wrap,' he said with a slight air of mystery as he assisted her into her seat.

She understood the reason for his comment later when he parked the car on the harbour front beside a gaily-lit double-decker ferry. 'All the tourists do it.' He gave a half grin escorting her on board.

He looked immense in evening dress, the white of his shirt front casting something of a glow on his craggy features as they stood together on the top deck under the night sky. Other people came up to enjoy the view and when the ferry was filled with laughing, chattering passengers it began its gliding journey across the bay.

Eve could see why the trip would appeal to visitors. Within a few minutes the whole twinkling harbour of Fort-de-France was encircled by its backcloth of starlit sable mountains, while the dark cut-outs of tall palm trees seemed to dwarf all but a few of the illuminated city buildings. On the breeze drifted the scent of spices, simmering sugar-cane and the multifarious blossoms on this island of flowers.

The aircraft designer drew her attention to where the lights of cruise ships were reflected in the glistening waters. 'Probably half the people on board tonight are on a busman's holiday from one of those.' He gleamed, draping the silver stole around her bare shoulders.

For the rest of the twenty minute ride neither spoke,

though there was plenty of gaiety in the background. From where they stood at the rail Eve was rooted by the loveliness of the jewelled bay, the soft mantle of night giving it a magic that no sunlit day could match.

A taxi was waiting for them when they docked, and a short while later Eve was alighting beside a mammoth edifice whose brilliantly lit foyer could have housed a small hotel in one corner, or so it seemed. Guiding her across the vast expanse of carpeted interior her escort was clearly no stranger here for several of the staff acknowledged him with smiling respect in passing.

The restaurant had been designed with a nightclub atmosphere. Several tiers of lamplit tables followed the curve of the dance floor around which were arranged the more exclusive tables. Towards one of these the dark-skinned *maître d'hôtel* led the way and Eve was noticing the expensive clientele in the various stages of dining.

Their own meal ordered by the man beside her, was typically Creole, starting with cream of coconut soup served in the husk, and ending with diced cantaloupe in syrup. By the time they had finished their second glass of French wine the dancing was in full swing.

Like the deck of a ship, the dance floor stretched out into the open under the stars. And unlike the modern parquet discos brought into fashion by the discotheque cult there was room for all. Perhaps the intimate atmosphere of treading on everyone else's feet or nudging and being nudged from all directions was devised for shy people, but Eve saw no reticent couples moving over the adequate polished space. It was a slightly different story for herself when her table companion led her on to the floor and took her into his arms.

The piercing pleasure of his nearness weakened her body momentarily, but supported against him her feet finally found the rhythm of his own. Of course he was a polished performer on the dance floor. His background was such that he had probably squired the most beautiful and elegant of London's society women around in this way. Eve was not sure whether her village hall prowess would suffice but though her partner guided her with confidence he demonstrated no energetic flair and she found the gentle sway of his muscular frame restful and almost hypnotic.

Few words had passed between them all evening. She had commented on the striking decor of the nightclub and he had explained why one of the dishes served to them during the meal comprising of green bananas, cod and sweet potatoes was called locally *ti nin lan morue*. But the preference to just muse along in the party atmosphere seemed mutual.

They danced most of the time. An orchestra on a dais amid blossoming shrubs played new songs and old. Eve found herself humming familiar snatches in her mind, melodies of the days long gone which her aunt had loved and known by heart. Towards the end of the evening they were dancing a beguine. 'Recognise the tune they're playing?' her partner asked.

'Of course.' She smiled. 'Cole Porter was my aunt's favourite songwriter.'

'A stock title on any Caribbean musician's list,' he told her between steps.

'Why is that?' She looked at him with humour. 'To indulge the more mature among the clientele?'

'That and the fact that the tourists expect it,' he explained. 'The American composer may have immortalised the beguine for us Anglo-Saxons, but the actual rhythm, the one danced by the Creole men and women hereabouts, started right here in Martinique. It's a little more sophisticated these days but it's thought to have first come from the Congo.' His arm tightening about her waist he whirled her into an intricate step. 'And that's about the only snippet of folklore I'm prepared to offer this evening,' he said.

Eve caught the gleam of his white smile in the shadows, but it wasn't music to whirl by, it was beaty and insistent and intimate and under the stars they moved as one, among the other couples, feeling no haste to cover more than an inch at a time over the floor.

Over on the brightly lit dais a young man with tawny good looks, dressed in white satin blouse and trousers with jewelled cummerbund was giving a sensitive rendering of the song.

'When they begin the beguine
It brings back a sound of music so tender
It brings back a night of tropical splendour
It brings back a memory ever dear . . .'

Eve listened and though poignantly of her aunt, a hard-working woman who had reaped little reward from life. But most of all she thought of the man who held her in his arms now and a wave of feeling so devastating in its sweetness brought stars to her soft, averted gaze which would have matched any in the velvet heavens above.

They left the glow of the dais behind and moved little by little down to the far end of the dance floor where night-shrouded gardens stretched in perfumed stillness. There were few couples here, phantom figures like themselves moving in the dream world of sentimental music and sound. Was it a dream Eve asked herself or were her partner's lips brushing her scented hair? Did she hear him murmuring urgently close to her 'Eve! Eve!' or was it just the words of the song playing tricks with her heart?

It was not the kind of music to spin and whirl to, but her senses whirled; reeled and reeled under the stars while her feet moved delicately and sedately to the beguine rhythm.

CHAPTER NINE

THERE were few passengers on the return ferry trip though the bay was as gaily lit as ever despite the late hour. The big man said during the crossing, 'You'll need your hiking shoes tomorrow. I'm going to take you for a stroll on Mount Pelee.'

'The one that erupted?' Eve asked, loving the warm sea breeze on her face.

'It's given a couple of puffs since its mammoth tantrum in nineteen hundred and two.' He smiled. 'But I was thinking of the view. In clear weather it's possible to see almost the whole of Martinique from up there.'

Later when he had dropped her outside the *pension* he returned to the subject by telling her. 'I'll be tied up tomorrow until about three. But I'll be along then to pick you up. Don't try the climb on your own before then,' he added in his dry way. 'You're likely to come off worse than you did with my guard dogs.'

The next morning found Eve in the heart of the city. Laconically Rydal Grantham had taken it upon himself to steer her clear of difficulties by escorting her around the island. But there were times, like now, when he had personal business to attend to. On these occasions she would spend the hours as far away from the Pension Desirade as possible.

It was ironic. In the early days her plan had been to avoid the aircraft designer. Now she had a fear of running into Rex. But one thing she didn't take into account where her brother was concerned. He was a past master at extracting information, or running it to earth. And he ran her to earth while she was ordering some scant refreshment at her midday haunt, a sidewalk cafe on the harbour front.

He slid into a chair beside her and removed his straw trilby with all the aplomb of someone keeping a previously arranged date. 'You can't fulfil newspaper assignments on a roll and mineral water,' he said grandly, snapping his fingers at a nearby waiter.

Ignoring his expansive mood Eve said, 'You forget you've left me practically penniless these past days.'

'Well now you've earned a slap-up meal,' he answered, smilingly unrepentant. 'Here's the menu. Take your choice.'

She accepted the bill of fare from the waiter and studied it while trying to still her thudding heart. The courses were simple and hardly top cuisine, but Rex was doing his best to appear magnanimous and she had no need to ask herself why.

During the meal, while they were engaged in small talk, she concentrated with her mind on the view; the sloops, ketches and freighters dotting the sparkling blue harbour; the sidewalk passers-by, a motley collection of Creole fishermen and dockworkers, camera and binocular-decked tourists and colourfully dressed country folk excitedly visiting from some rural village.

She would have liked to keep her attention more or less fixed with the beautiful, tawny-skinned faces of the townspeople who passed by their table but towards the coffee stage Rex said, his grin slightly taut, 'Well, don't keep me in suspense, Eve. What's new? I take it you've got quite a bit to report on the Grantham front?'

Eve carefully folded her napkin. 'I can't really tell you much except that I've become something of an authority on the island of Martinique.'

She had resorted to flippancy as a means of escaping Rex's scrutiny but if anything it only intensified his knife-edge mood. From the benevolent brother he became the implacable, ambitious young journalist.

'Don't string me along, Sis,' he said between set teeth. 'You've had enough time now to milk the whole damn story from Grantham.'

'I told you at the start I was no good for the job.' Eve kept her eyes on the strollers. 'I'm not a . . . milker, as you call it. I'll never make one of your beguiling female news dredgers.'

'Well you'd better start learning how to.' His face had paled with anger. 'We've got two days to break this thing wide open. And I think I told you at the start. We're not going home without the story that's going to put me on top in my career.'

Eve remembered well enough all that the aircraft man had revealed to her regarding his work; why he had walked out of the board meeting and more, but it had been told to her in trust and she would never, never divulge it to anyone.

'I . . . can't promise,' she stammered through constricted throat. 'We're friends . . . Good friends, I suppose . . .' *Dear God what an understatement that was where her happy, aching heart was concerned!* 'But friends don't talk about . . .' She didn't finish. The words she had been about to speak froze on her lips for moving along the sidewalk with the crowd, coming directly this way past their table was a figure which in the last two or more weeks had grown considerably familiar to her.

As she had learned, a top man in the aircraft world with Rydal Grantham's talents, who was currently causing eruptions in the news media with his spectacular disappearance, could not afford to go anywhere without adequate protection from the press and public. His 'henchmen' as Rex called them were by this time well-known to her, having seen them somewhere in the background on practically every outing she had taken with their employer, on the island.

Now she was looking into the face of one of them, a sprucely dressed, dark-skinned islander of about forty, whose educated aura did not detract from his massive, pugilistic build. He was accompanied by a good-looking woman around his own age, undoubtedly his wife, and as bodyguards take time off like any other man who earns his living, they were clearly in Fort-de-France on a week-end outing.

Almost as soon as she had spotted him Eve averted her gaze and pretended to drink deep from her coffee cup. Had he seen her? A pulse hammered behind her eyes so strung up were her nerves, but when he had passed she told herself that with the tables crowded as they were on this Sunday afternoon, and so many people filing along the sidewalk, it was hardly likely that he would have noticed much as he went by.

It had all happened in a matter of seconds and taking up where she had left off, as though she had simply been searching for the right words she concluded in considerably more strained tones, '. . . friends don't talk about . . . mundane professional ups and downs.'

'Look.' Rex leaned in, in his grim-faced intense way. 'You don't think I can keep this thing to myself forever do you? I knew when we came out here that sooner or later Grantham's whereabouts would be stumbled upon, and sure enough news-hungry pressmen from both sides of the Atlantic are on to the scent. The island's crawling with optimistic story-hounds, but I got here first and I don't intend to lose that lead.' He rose and tossed money on to the table to pay for the meal, adding beneath his breath as a parting shot, 'I've got you nicely entrenched in Grantham's confidence and I want action. Action and the goods.'

She watched him walk off and disappear among the strollers her face white with conflicting emotions.

When the man so much in pursuit by the press and Rex came to pick her up at three outside the *pension* she had all but managed to overcome the effects of that scene with her brother. But perhaps traces of the ordeal she had been through at the sidewalk cafe table still showed in her face for when they had stopped on their first rest up the mountain the aeronautic expert's keen blue gaze, she felt, was taking in the pale transparency of her skin, her faintly shadowed eyes.

'You look about as robust as one of Ignace's shaved sugar sticks, after your holiday,' he said a little gratingly. 'Maybe I should have advised you to lie in the shade all day rather than show you the real Martinique.'

'I've enjoyed it.' She smiled. 'It's done me the world of good.' She could never have got tired of visiting and driving around at this man's side. What had exhausted her was striving to keep him and her brother Rex apart in her mind and apart from each other. But it was almost over now. Tomorrow she would die a little. *A little!* Her heart would cease to beat for any other man as long as she lived. That much she knew. But she would, by this time tomorrow, have said her last goodbyes to him, and Rex would leave without ever knowing how much it had cost her to put this hard-jawed semi-stranger before her affection for him.

But that was tomorrow. At the moment she wanted to forget her brother's shadow over the day and so she suggested lightly, 'Just to prove how fit I am I'll race you up the mountain.'

'There are no rest houses along the way,' her companion said sternly, 'and my beach bungalow divan is not immediately available for collapsing women tourists who bite off more than they can chew. This is a four thousand feet ascent.' However he took her hand and they swung along together over uneven ground.

He was wearing rough slacks and a light sweater over his open-necked shirt. On his advice Eve had dressed for cool breezes too. Her tweed walking skirt, fleecy blouse and lilac waistcoat were ample against the rarefied air.

She had been collected from the *pension* in a jeep and they had driven up a good portion of the mountain in this sturdy machine before resorting to foot. Now they trod through a knee-high mantle of yellowing ferns. Away from the path, littered by black-shelled snails, cabbage-like cacti put up strange blue flowers and huge grey crickets whirred up at the disturbance.

At last they arrived on level ground atop a great lava shoulder. Pausing to rest they looked down on scarves of mist caught between sun-warmed peaks. The resurrected town of St Pierre obliterated by the eruption at the turn of the century, claiming twenty-nine thousand lives, lay at their feet along the Caribbean. Eve had read in the tourist literature that only one man had survived the holocaust, a prisoner in a thick-walled dungeon, who for years afterwards was displayed abroad as a circus attraction and lived to the ripe old age of eighty-two. How strange fate was she mused to herself, weaving human destiny in this way. And capricious chance always there to put a twist in the tail.

Take her own life for instance. Who would have thought that after years in a sleepy English village she would develop a strong attraction for a tropical island in another hemisphere? The twist in her case of course was that she had discovered a love deep in herself for a man who belonged not of her world, and who once her holiday was at an end, she could never see again. Having Rex for a relative prevented any extension of a friendship which had been fostered, albeit indirectly, by her brother.

After the breather they crossed a narrow ridge connecting the lava mass to Pelee's upper slope. Wisps of cloud blurred the route. The snail shells crunched under their feet. Hurrying on, keen for the thrill of reaching the summit Eve was stopped by an urgent arm about her waist. 'Slow down,' the big man warned her.

'There's a sheer drop of a couple of hundred feet from the brink of the crater.'

Pausing in the curve of his arm she was sobered not just by his words but by their complete isolation from the outside world. A rising mist swirling at their feet, there were no neat-clothed guardians of privacy here; no family members at a visited plantation keeping them apart. A wind moaned over the rock-strewn landscape and somehow Rydal Grantham's expression was in keeping with the desolation.

As they approached the fern-fringed edge of the gaping crater, now grassed over and mossy, curved symmetrically away on either side. Green to the top, two domes jutted several hundred feet above the crater rim obscuring the islands north tip, but the rest of Martinique lay below them, a miniature kingdom of green fields, blue mountains and bluer coves. The red-roofed houses of the towns were matchbox neat, the waves on the beaches like fine french lace over aquamarine silk.

The big man pointed out to her Diamond Rock out at sea, a village with the amusing title of Deux Choux— Two Cabbages, and the vast fertile stretches of sugar-cane, bananas and citrus trees. For some considerable time they stood with their own thoughts above the view. But Eve's attention turned once again to St Pierre and just then the town's church bells reached them faintly and sadly she thought. Time was running out for her. But she couldn't leave without first knowing that this man was at last at peace with himself.

He was pointing to the bare volcanic slopes. 'I imagine that's how the mountain got its name,' he theorised. 'Pelee means bald in french.'

They turned back to the view and in the long pause that followed she asked, watching him, 'Have you found the solution to your problem?'

'Yes.' His gaze toured the coastline. 'I've made my

decision.' The wind lifted dark strands of his hair. His profile seemed a fraction short of its usual invincibility. Touched by the flaw her love for him detected in his powerful make-up she asked, 'May I know what it is?'

'I'll tell you tomorrow.' He smiled, taking her arm for the descent.

Tomorrow was her last day but he made no mention of this on the drive back. Outside the *pension* he simply said, 'I'll pick you up at two,' and with a nod drove off into the violet dusk.

Eve spent the evening packing. The following morning she walked the streets around the market place. Rex wouldn't find her here and a few more hours would see the end of this hide and seek nightmare. He had no choice but return to England tomorrow she knew, and her heart was wrung at the terrible disappointment he would have to take back with him. But there was no compassion in her that would move her to do as he asked. She was a woman who's visions and emotions had moved beyond the bounds of brotherly love.

She gazed unseeingly at the Madras prints in the shops and wondered what the much-hunted aviation man had planned for this afternoon. The thought of spending her last few hours with him filled her with a mixture of radiant happiness and quiet despair. Could she go on in Ingledene when she returned? Or should she start a new life in another place; somewhere where Rex couldn't find her to remind her of these three weeks of heaven and hell?

She dressed carefully after lunch. She had only a simple wardrobe but as a last token before her soon-to-be bleak departure she wanted to look her best. Her apple-green sun-dress had faded with time but it was crisp and neat and high-lighted the russet tints of her softly waving hair. Sun hat in hand she went down and out to the kerb. Her eager eyes scanned the street for

the familiar car, but for the first time since she had
known him Rydal Grantham was late.

A glance at her watch told her it was seven minutes
past two. The traffic jams in Fort-de-France were
irksome but not usually at this hour. At two-fifteen he
came. She supposed he must have driven in a hurry for
he pulled up beside her with an uncharacteristic
shrieking of brakes.

'Get in.' As he leaned across to open the door she
wondered if some mild upset in his normally cast-iron
constitution had caused his delay. His features were a
putty grey colour, and though a smile was noticeable on
his lips his face appeared mask-like in the confines of
the car.

They shot away and she took to wondering again if
they were behind in some travelling schedule. Perhaps
he had planned a special afternoon with a French
colonial family and didn't want to appear rude by
arriving late.

Within minutes they had left the town behind and
were hurtling through the countryside. But Rydal was a
skilful driver and Eve relaxed in her seat and mused on
the cultivated stretches of breadfruit, custard apple and
avocado flanking the road. However, when she saw that
they were making for the Atlantic side of the island she
asked, pleasurably curious, 'Where are we going?'

'To my house. I thought as I've never taken you there
you'd like that.' The smile with which he had greeted
her outside the *pension* still sloped his lips tightly, and
the glitter in his eyes must have been the reflection of
the sunshine through the windscreen.

In a way Eve didn't know whether to be glad or sorry
that they were going to spend the afternoon alone.
Naturally she wanted to see the domain where Rydal
retired to from the world when he was on the island,
but it might have been easier, for her at least, if he had
chosen to embroil them both in some social plantation

gathering for their farewell outing. She kept her gaze with the view, half of her praying for plane time tomorrow, the other half wishing the afternoon could go on and on into eternity.

The land was now taken up with banana groves. She remembered the route from that first drive with Rex, but of course she had seen nothing of the house then, hadn't known one existed. And shortly she was to see why. They took a track which appeared to lead nowhere but within a few minutes came upon a drive entrance almost hidden by jungle-like greenery.

Some electronics system must have been incorporated in the wrought-iron gates for Rydal pressed a bleep signal in his car and at once they opened. Though wild on the outside, the grounds she saw as they approached from the drive were neatly laid out and a riot of colour. There were tropical plants and shrubbery here that she hadn't known existed. Great shell-pink trumpets festooned one end of the brick-roofed veranda while tubs of giant peonies stood at the base of each pillar. The lawns and house, a rambling structure of rustic design, were enclosed by a thick forest of trees which looked as impenetrable as fortress walls.

All was quiet in the grounds and privately Eve wondered where the guard personnel were stationed. She supposed that as unobtrusive as always they were somewhere in the background observing without being seen.

The car had come to a stop at the end of the driveway. Rydal left his seat and strode round to open her door. 'The gardens are kept in trim by a couple of veteran Creoles.' He waved an arm to indicate the blossoms and greenery with uncharacteristic expansiveness she thought. 'And this is the veranda.' He led the way, eyeing the items of lounging furniture, the personal touches as though to highlight each piece for her benefit.

'And now we have the indoors.' He turned and bowed for her to precede him. He was not a man given to flamboyant gestures and Eve could only assume that he was over-exaggerating his guide role to lighten the task of admitting a visitor to his private world. And undoubtedly that glitter in his eyes would be doused when they left the sunlight.

The interior was very masculine in an expensive sort of way. The solid gleaming furniture, she guessed, was of French design. And there were art pieces in this spacious living room that even her untrained eye told her were exclusive and maybe priceless. But the focal point of the room was the view looking out through a gap in the trees to the blue ocean, infinite horizons and a section of the blossom-framed beach.

'It's quite beautiful,' she murmured sincerely.

'But it's only the start.' He strode over the parquet flooring flinging doors open. 'There are eight rooms in all. This is the library . . . Over here we have the dining room . . . The kitchen faces north, like all good kitchens . . . and the bedrooms . . .'

Following him in one direction and then the other, Eve demurred, 'I don't think it's necessary to——'

'But I want you to see *everything*,' he cut in, moving through the house. 'You never know, you may have to describe what colour breakfast cup I take my coffee in; if I use an electric razor or the good old-fashioned cut-throat.' He opened a door. 'This is the master bedroom, mine of course. As you can see I like to read in bed—oh, and I sometimes take a snorter of whisky . . . The guest rooms are this way. I don't go in for entertaining out here, but occasionally I have a couple of guests . . .'

Amidst the blur of gleaming and adequately furnished rooms Eve was trying to focus her mind on the breakfast cup comment. She couldn't get it to make sense, nor could she fathom the motive for this rather hectic house tour. 'There's really no need to . . .' she trailed off with a puzzled laugh. But as though she had not spoken he kept up his running commentary while pointing to secluded niches and passageways. 'I have an Indian cook. A valet who comes from nearby Barbados. The house is run by a Corobrier couple . . .'

As they approached the living room once more Eve began to feel a chilly apprehension. There was something not right here. Rydal had never been one for out and out gaiety, but his taut, joking mood now was laced with something close to buffoonery. If it had been just that she would have put it down to one of the hidden facets of his nature that she was not yet familiar with. But there was a kind of leashed control about his movements, a savage slant to his ever-present smile that gripped her in the pit of her stomach.

'Now, how about a drink?' He moved to a cabinet in the mellow room and opened it with not too steady a hand so that the bottles were displayed. 'What would you like? Something heavy like the shot I gave you when you swooned on my beach? Or a nip of our good old *ti* punch?'

Eve felt a terrible desolation as she spoke. 'If I'm a nuisance here, I don't mind if you drive me back to town.'

'So soon!' His surprise was theatrical. 'Aren't you going to ask me what colour socks I like and when I last visited my barber?'

'Why should I want to do that?' She was beginning to picture herself as an ineffectual mouse fencing off the attentions of a wickedly playful cat.

'Because that's your job.' He picked up a bottle and uncorked it. 'You like to know how creative recluses like me tick.'

'You know my job,' she said quietly while icy fingers closed round her heart. 'I sell newspapers on a village high street.'

'You sell them, or you write them?' He lifted a glass

up to the light and measured the liquid in it with eyes, she saw, that glittered far worse than they had done in the sunshine. 'Or is it that brother of yours who does the penmanship while you attend to the finer details of gaining the confidence of the current meat package for the market?'

Eve knew her face had turned to alabaster. 'How long have you known about Rex?' she asked.

'Since this morning,' came the crisp reply. 'He was seen talking to you at a harbour-side cafe table on Sunday. Lazus, one of my men, who has spent the time since checking him out both here and in Britain, discovered that he's one of the most rabied freelancers ever to graduate from the printers ink colony of leeches, better known as pressmen.'

Eve's cheeks, blanched and too frozen to burn at the vitriolic comment, she said, 'I'm sorry you had to know.'

'Yes, it's touching isn't it?' He measured out liquor in a second glass. 'The work you must have put in to get as far as you did, and then to have the whole thing shot to bits by a chance stroll by an off-duty vigilante of mine.'

Rex! Rex! She cried out in her mind. Why did you have to get careless at the end? She knew of course that she had more or less driven him to it by evading him. And he had become too desperate for news about Rydal in the latter days to care much about whether he was seen or not.

Over her wildly racing heart she heard the relentless voice in the room continuing in an almost chatty manner. 'I'll admit you were convincing. The way you buckled prettily at the sight of my guard dogs. And running straight into my arms the night of the Corobrier festival. You were good as the bungling tourist. I wanted to put you straight on a few things by showing you over the island and you played the perfect

travelling companion, even lending an ear to the trials of
my working life as a good travelling companion would.'

His satire was belied only by his ashen features. Eve
was fixed by the molten steel in his gaze as surely as if
she had been a moth pinned by an inexorable flame. He
was convinced that she had deceived him. How could
she tell him that none of it was the way it looked? Even
Rex believed she had followed his instructions. She had
striven to rid herself of the net of intrigue he had woven
for her and only succeeded in sealing herself in from
escape. How could she explain to Rydal that her getting
to know him had all been the result of trying to *avoid*
him? He would never believe her. And how could she
expect him to? Feeling his disappointments and
frustrations as strongly as though they were her own,
and wanting to know about his work and to help by
listening, she couldn't have made a more damning alias
for herself if she had tried.

'Oh yes, you were good,' he went on. 'I've met some
armour-plated charmers in my time but you acted the
part like a natural. You played hard to get just long
enough to stimulate my moth-balled chivalry at your
cock-eyed way of seeing the island . . .'

'You're talking as if I'm some sort of "siren",' she
had to cut in, 'when really I'm only——'

'We know what kind of woman you are, Eve.' He
approached her slowly. 'Gentle, unsophisticated, comradely and clever. Here, have a drink.'

She looked at the glass in his hand. 'Wouldn't it be
better if I went right now?' she said in a lifeless voice.
'I'll be on the plane tomorrow.'

'You're not leaving the island or this house for the
time being.' He thrust the drink at her and in a stupid
way she took it. 'Sit down.' He indicated a chair. 'Let's
be matey, shall we, while we discuss what I should do to
get even.'

CHAPTER TEN

SHE lowered herself because the effect of his deadly anger together with her churning emotions had robbed her of the capacity to stand.

'Your brother ... Rex, isn't it? Rex Bowen, the columnist who always gets his scoop.' He gave her his corrosive smile. 'He's carved quite a niche for himself I believe, with the daily papers. But you know,' from studying the contents of his glass the glittering blue eyes lifted to meet hers, 'I could strip him of his feathers overnight.'

Eve, already white-faced, shrunk a little in her seat. Hiding her anguish she said, 'Rex has worked hard to get where he is.'

'By fair means or foul, eh?'

'I'll admit his methods are sometimes a little unethical,' she replied palely, 'but newsmen too have to eat.'

'True,' he conceded. 'And taking it as a whole he has kept out of my way whereas you have made damn sure—in your inimitable fumbling style of course—that you got in it.' He looked at her, his grey features contorted by that smile. 'You'll agree that I'm entitled to extract vengeance in any way I choose for being duped by your charm as the gentle confidante. And even if you don't agree, that's the way I work.' Ponderingly he added, 'Your brother Rex may or may not be deprived of his meal ticket. We shall have to see.'

Completely shattered Eve said in a small firm voice, 'And what punishment do you reckon fits my behaviour?'

103

He threw the rest of his drink back, placed the glass down unhurriedly and replied, 'Marriage—with me.'

If Eve hadn't been seated her legs would have given way at the shock. As it was the room spun a little and she gripped the arms of her chair to shake off the feeling of unreality. 'I . . . I don't understand.' Her voice too sounded unreal.

'It's perfectly simple.' He paced, his anger all omnipotent, his gaze averted. 'I need a wife. It may not be noticeable here in Martinique, but in Europe I'm what is known as an eligible bachelor, and there are women, as you probably know despite your pose as the rustic *ingénue*,' he shot her his razor-edged grin, 'who will stop at nothing to achieve their ambitions in the marriage market.'

Watching him in the room, his controlled wrath making him a man of steel, she mentioned candidly, 'I would have thought you more than capable of stemming the flow of admiration from the opposite sex.'

'I am.' He smiled decisively. 'But it's time-consuming, whereas you will nicely eliminate those pressures and leave me free to concentrate on my work.'

'Are you suggesting that I act as a buffer between you and . . .?'

'A formidable army of caustic-minded, velvet-tongued females of varying beauty, wit and skill in the art of getting a man? I'm afraid so.' He put on a look of mocking apology and shrugged, 'It would be like being thrown to the lions for some, but you, dear Eve, should manage quite well.'

Wretchedly she met his gaze. Though he was a stranger to her like this, ruthless, cruel, vindictive, she still loved him. 'And what if I refuse to marry you?' she asked in a dead voice.

'Then dear Rex will be de-feathered,' came the bland reply. 'It would be simple. He wants a story. I could invite him here and give him the interview he desires. I could tell him things about my work that would start his journalistic mouth watering. But there wouldn't be a word of truth in it. And when he got back to England and splashed the interview in his column he would be the laughing stock of Fleet Street because the other papers would have, by then, the correct version of my rapid withdrawal from the commercial aeronautical scene.'

She said through drained lips, 'You wouldn't be so vile?'

'You don't know me as well as you thought you did, Eve.' He gleamed brutally. 'I can do this and much, much more. On the other hand,' he paused significantly, almost lazily, 'I could ask your brother here, give him all the genuine information he's straining for; an interview that would no doubt establish his authority in the press world. But it would have to be on the understanding that you are to be my wife.'

His wife. At the thought Eve knew both rapture and desolation. As an act of vengeance he was tying her to him for life—or until he tired of her. But she would have gladly died right now if there had been a spark of affection in his proposal.

'Very well,' she said in a hollow voice. 'To save my brother from professional annihilation I'll do as you stipulate.'

Where he stood, a little way from her, his face was partly in shadow but it seemed as though a great weariness overtook him at her reply, then he was saying in typical malicious vein, 'I thought you would see it my way. Now if you would care to follow me,' with a finger he pressed a bell nearby, 'I'll ask Duco to show you to a guest room. We will be married as soon as possible but in the meantime there is sufficient staff around the house to maintain an air of respectability during your pre-marital stay.'

Eve rose. 'I . . . I'll need to fetch my things from the pension,' she said faintly.

'That won't be necessary.' Again that corrosive smile. 'One of my men can go and pick up your possessions.'

Did he think that she would try and escape him? How little he knew of her true feelings. She was as incapable of running from him now as she had been of saying no to being with him when he had offered to show her the island at the start.

'How . . . will you contact Rex?' she asked as they went out.

'His whereabouts have been known to me ever since he was first seen in your company,' came the suave reply. 'I shall invite him here now, this afternoon. The interview will take some time so I would advise you to rest. I shall say nothing of our . . . bargain. Simply that you have agreed to become my wife. You will have a chance to speak with your brother before he leaves.'

Beyond the living room a thick-set West Indian in white jacket appeared through a doorway not included in the 'tour' of the house. 'Ah, Duco, I want you to meet a guest of mine. Miss Bowen. Eve Bowen. Would you show her to a room and see that she has every comfort.' She was preparing to move off mechanically when he added, 'Miss Bowen is my fiancée, Duco. We are to be married quite soon.'

The servant accepted this piece of news as though long since tuned to the disciplinarian commands and whims of his employer. Grizzled-haired with a pleasant dark-skinned face he said in the deep, musical tones of the locality, 'May I offer my congratulations, sir.'

'There you are, Eve.' She was fixed by a hard blue gaze filled with secret contempt and even amusement. 'Our first well-wisher for our future happiness.'

'Thank you, Duco.' She smiled, though inwardly she felt like death. So this was what she could expect from Rydal in the future. His searing scorn and private hate while he made a show of being suavely entranced by her company in the presence of others. He believed that she had cheated him just as those in his professional life had let him down. He must feel that there was no one he could trust. But did he have to be so merciless with her?

The room she was shown into was one she had admired earlier but now she viewed the beautiful French-style furnishings and forest views from the windows with a lack-lustre eye. For long enough she moved about the suite touching things without seeing, her mind filled with the torment of the past hour, and all her fears now centred around Rex. What if something happened between them to make Rydal go back on his word? What if he planned to ruin her brother anyway, as he had threatened to do at the start? She was entirely at his mercy not knowing which of the two choices open to him he would take. But he had her as hostage and the bargain was that it was her skin for Rex's.

Reasonably satisfied that her brother at least would come out of it all unscathed she fell at last, through sheer emotional exhaustion, on the bed. Though her body throbbed and that drained feeling gave her the impression she was ill, she slipped after a while into a fretful slumber.

It was a knock on the door which roused her. Thinking that it was Duco and that he would move off after alerting her, she lay for some moments struggling up from the mists of sleep. She was just raising her head from the pillow when the door opened and Rydal strode in.

He eyed her coldly where she lay, his smile as unpleasant as ever. 'Your brother is waiting, to say goodbye,' he said levelly.

Giddily she swung her feet to the floor feeling that a little privacy would have been preferable at a time like this. Though acutely embarrassed at being found lying prone by him she wanted to laugh hysterically at the thought. What privacy could she expect from her husband-to-be? Clearly he was determined to let her see from the start that she was his now in every sense of the word.

She went to tidy her hair at the mirror. He watched her through narrowed lids. He was enjoying her embarrassment as he meant to enjoy every humiliation she suffered at his hands. She was alarmed at the stark white face that stared back at her, but with a look of composure she turned and indicated that she was ready to follow him.

Rex rose when she entered a room gay with roses in a vase and late afternoon sunshine. She knew at once by his flushed features and shining eyes that he was immensely pleased. 'Eve, this surpasses anything I ever dreamed of!' He hugged her briefly. 'How did you do it?'

'Did the interview go as you expected it to?' she asked anxiously.

'I didn't expect the red carpet treatment but that's what I got,' he laughed. 'Grantham bent over backwards to be accommodating. I never knew he had charm as well as brains. The story he's given me is a beaut. Everything on his career so far—warts an' all as they say. And it's all in here.' He patted a brief-case in his hand. 'Taped and ready to roll as soon as I can get it down on paper.'

'I'm glad you got what you wanted,' Eve said, battling to hide her low spirits. 'I take it you'll be flying home tomorrow?'

'I wish I could go tonight,' he grinned. 'I'm so excited I could practically sprout wings and do the trip solo.' He looked momentarily abashed. 'I'd like to stay for the wedding, Sis, but you know how it is, business and all that.'

She hoped he wouldn't notice her shattered expression

but he was in a talkative mood and not a little bewildered. 'When Grantham told me he'd asked you to be his wife I thought he was taking the mickey at my nose for news. Here was me thinking that you were playing it cool every step of the way and now . . . this?' He shrugged happily perplexed, then shot her a cryptic gleam, 'I suppose you know you've made the catch of the season. Grantham's royalties on his plane designs have made him a millionaire several times over, and he may be no Gregory Peck but he has a string of female followers who have had their eye on his bank balance for some time . . .'

She let her brother's hearty chat wash over her. If he stopped to think about it, a proposal of marriage within three weeks of her knowing the man was rather odd. But Eve knew that Rex was not the type to think deeply about anything except his own ambitions. Nor did he care whether she was happy or not. He simply wanted to get back to the scene of his work, which was his life.

Already fidgeting he glanced at his watch. 'I ought to be pushing along now, Eve. I still have to pack and I want to make a couple of 'phone calls concerning these.' He tapped his brief-case again. 'But I'll be in touch with you some time and you can let me know how you're making out in your tropical paradise with money to burn. Some people have all the luck!' With his shallow humour he dropped a kiss on her cheek. 'So long, Eve, and take care.'

'Goodbye, Rex, I hope that . . .' But he hadn't heard. A chauffered car was waiting for him beyond the veranda and rapidly negotiating the steps he climbed inside without a backward glance and was driven off.

Disconsolately Eve turned back into the room not quite knowing what to do next. She didn't feel she had sufficient run of the house to freely retrace her steps to the suite she had been provided with. And the gardens though apparently deserted were probably watched over by unseen eyes. Her quandary was resolved for her by the appearance of Rydal. He came into the room giving the impression that he had been somewhere nearby most of the time.

'Before dinner we'd better discuss our wedding plans,' he said, as though suggesting a chat about the weather. 'You realise of course that this will make you the star attraction for the newsmen who have descended on the island having discovered my whereabouts. I shall try to protect you from this nuisance wherever possible, but a certain amount of publicity will, I think, be inevitable. You will need clothes . . . a bridal outfit . . .' She felt that his lips twisted for she was not looking his way. 'It would be impossible to purchase these things ourselves. We would be mobbed if we attempted it in downtown Fort-de-France. I suggest we have you fitted out here in the house. I myself will supervise your wardrobe. I shall also put plans into motion for the wedding ceremony and the reception. In the meantime feel free to wander where you please. The house is yours. The beach.' That slope to the hard mouth again, she was sure. 'The grounds make pleasant walking. You will not be interfered with in any way, simply protected from prying eyes.'

He paused as though waiting for her to comment. Her throat was too constricted to speak. To be the object of his hate and contempt was more than she could bear when her whole being cried out to be loved by him.

'Your brother, by the way,' she heard him fill the silence, 'has been given the first and only insight into my private working life. It's all bona-fide stuff and there's no risk of him falling flat on his face in front of his readers.' Again the pause.

When Eve could find her voice she said 'Thank you for that.'

In the stillness of the room it seemed to her that for

the second time that afternoon he shrunk somehow in stature as she spoke. But almost at once that icy disdain had taken over his tones and he was concluding, 'Your suitcase has arrived so you will be able to change for dinner. The staff will expect us to display a little bit of style for our engagement supper. Why not put on that silver thing for the occasion?'

The dress she had worn the night of the beguine. The night her heart had soared as high as the stars they danced beneath. Oh how cruel could he get! He was extracting atonement for the unforgivable double game he believed she had played, but if only he knew that he was crucifying her in another way.

CHAPTER ELEVEN

THE evening meal was a farce of correct almost gay behaviour for the benefit of the staff with undertones of scorn and mockery which she alone was meant to detect in his manner. His conversation centred around all the trips they had made together on the island. He mentioned the sugar plantations and the homes of his friends in the hills they had visited and highlighted all the while, she noticed, the occasions when they had talked whilst admiring this view or that.

Oh, Eve knew what he was skilfully implying while presenting a lighthearted picture for the servants passing back and forth. But it wasn't true. None of it was true. She hadn't led him on simply so that she could carry all she had heard back to Rex. She had known tenderness and a passionate desire to comfort, that was why she had encouraged him to ease his mind with talk. But how could she ever get him to believe that? How could she ever make him see that he was wrong! Wrong! Horribly wrong about her?

The next two days passed in a whirl though Eve was too numbed both mentally and physically to react much to the commotion around her. Perhaps her mechanical air was taken for happy composure and an admirable lack of nerves, for she was viewed enchantedly as a wife-to-be and given the treatment that any fiancée of a wealthy man might expect in the way of grooming for the all-important moment.

Eve had had no occasion—being practically penniless most of her holiday—to shop in the smart section of the town; the exclusive stores and fashion houses along the Rues Victor Hugo and Antoine Siger. But she had

112

wandered around that vicinity when striving to avoid her brother or Rydal, and she had seen some of the elegant Parisian outfits, the perfumes, the footwear and expensive accessories in the glittering interiors.

Now such things were displayed for her by French speaking assistants, who in turn were supervised by a bird-like woman with a polish for clothes which was reflected in her own faultless attire and brittle but smilingly helpful manner.

As it happened Eve was not called upon to make many decisions during the fittings. Rydal either approved or disapproved. He chose for her dresses and cloque hats, cocktail ensembles, evening wear and outdoor clothes. With a pain she realised he knew her better than she knew herself when it came to the matters of dress. There was simplicity in the styles he picked; nothing heavy or dramatic. They were clothes that she knew instinctively were right for her.

But when it came to her wedding outfit the ageing couturier threw up her hands and protested in the most voluble French. Rydal explained with a cryptic grin apparently meant only for Eve. Which, of course, she knew it was as he explained, 'Madame Jacline is trying to point out that a bridegroom should not see his bride's outfit until the moment of the ceremony. It's supposed to be terribly unlucky for our future life together.'

'I'm not superstitious,' Eve said, thinking that this was the easiest way around the hold-up.

'Nor am I,' he replied impassively, 'but I think we'll indulge the woman on this point. I can just as well take myself off to some other part of the house while she gets to work on you.' As he went out he added, 'She's a shrewd judge of character, is Madame. She'll size you up well for the occasion, you can rely on it.'

Always taunting her with what he believed had been her dual role in his life. Eve swallowed on her misery.

He never missed a chance to be ruthless where he could despite his thoughtful generosity as a husband-to-be.

When she wasn't needed for preparations for the wedding Eve spent most of her time out of doors. She went alone to the beach, paddled her feet as she had done that first afternoon, but wistfully now, and returned white-faced each time past the beach house en route. She met Lise and Clemane the middle-aged island couple who ran the house for Rydal, and at a distance one or two of the hand-picked security men who patrolled the land between the two headlands.

Everyone took to her, or accepted her as the woman their employer had chosen to be his wife. If only they knew! She would have given anything in the world if it had been genuinely so.

A French hairdresser came early on the day of the wedding. Whether Rydal had spoke to him first she didn't know, but once again there was no drastic change made in her appearance. Her hair was trimmed expertly but left at that. However, when everything else was done, she could feel that it was softer, shinier, more full-blown and wavier than before.

Madame Jacline arrived, and later dressed in a crêpe de Chine two piece in palest turquoise with a hat which framed her glowing hairstyle and softened her pallor with its veil, Eve's own impression was that nothing of her true personality had been tampered with. Rydal had said that Madame was a true judge of character. Would he himself, she wondered, approve of her appearance for the occasion?

To avoid publicity she would have thought that his main aim would be to keep things as private as possible. Instead she found herself being driven to a small chapel set in the surrounding banana plantations, where the ceremony was performed before a pew-packed interior. Later emerging into the sunlight, her pale features taken to be the result of suppressed excitement, they were showered with confetti—silver horseshoes, stars, crescent moons and roses she noticed with damp eyes—by the house staff and Rydal's friends.

He drove the car himself to the scene of the reception. The gold band feeling heavy and cold on her finger she sat in the seat beside him. He looked thinner though still immense in dark suit, white shirt and silver-grey tie. 'Brave yourself for the wolves, my dear,' he said with his hard smile. 'The jet-set season is in full swing in the West Indies, and half of London's society is putting up at the moment along this string of islands. Martinique has its share. They're falling over themselves to meet the new Mrs Rydal Grantham.'

He didn't point out that he had invited these people to the reception which of course he must have done. And Eve was inclined to amend his 'wolves' comment to smiling vixens when later she was surrounded by a bevy of sharply curious ladies all wanting to know, in jocular vein of course, how she managed to land one of the most dedicated bachelors ever to circulate their ranks.

The room of an expensive beach-side hotel given over to the reception could not have been lovelier if she had truly been chosen as Rydal's wife. Red and cream roses, sprays of mauve and white lilac imported from heaven knew where, decorated every space. The long buffet table besides being adorned by simple posies of flowers was filled with dainty french savouries, delicate pastries, glaced fruits and sweets, and had at its centre a four-tiered cake topped by a single white rose set in silver.

While West Indian hotel staff mingled among the guests with trays of champagne Eve was introduced here and there at Rydal's side. She met distinguished looking men, and their wives elegantly turned out in pastels for the occasion; pleasant people on the whole and charming towards Rydal if a little distant towards herself. But she found ease and comfort in the company of his other friends, island people like Ignace and Monique Guamel who embraced her affectionately. The older members of the family from the Lazaret plantation were looking extremely smart in suits and tailored dresses, as were the rest of the French settlers community. And the business people, the owners of the country houses she had visited in the past, were especially thrilled she noted, with a weight crushing her heart beneath her smile, to see her joined in matrimony to their favourite island recluse.

Rex had told her about the beautiful women in Rydal's life and there was no shortage of these at the reception, with or without male escorts. Masculine companionship or lack of it appeared to make no difference to the comments put forth by these sleek sun-seekers from her own northern clime.

One such lovely individual with shoulder-length dark hair and jade-green eyes pouted, 'It was mean of you, Rydal, to sneak out here without a word to any of us of what you intended. You know we would have adored to have been in on the big secret.'

Another blue-eyed blonde was openly bitter in a joking way. 'It's what you can expect from a man who never smiles with his eyes,' she commented. 'My mother always said to me never trust a man who doesn't smile with his eyes.'

But the most telling complaint to Eve's way of thinking—though it was not put like a complaint at all—came from a woman in a powder-blue suit leaning on the arm of a darkly handsome young man. About thirty years old, she had an exquisitely small-boned face, an enviable figure and provocative husky voice. 'Rydal always knows what he's doing,' she drawled. 'If he got married in a hurry then he must have his own good reasons.' It was a simple quip but skilfully underlined to suggest that not all men married for love.

Meeting the dark-fringed violet eyes behind this remark Eve had the feeling that there was a shrewdness here that could see right past her smile into her miserable interior. A little to her surprise she heard Rydal replying in the same lazy vein, 'You know me, Philippa. Never put a foot wrong. I appraise women like I appraise the qualities of a flying machine. I wouldn't want either of them to let me down.'

They moved on to more banter until it was time to cut the cake. Rydal's hand felt strong and cool over her own on the knife. If only she hadn't felt that the thrust was through her own heart. They smiled for the private camera enthusiasts and of course the press. It was while her brand new husband was humouring the newsmen with light chat concerning the occasion that Eve found herself alone beside the buffet table. But not for long. While she listened detached to the babble in the room she was joined by a thin, mature woman with cinnamon coloured hair and a business-like friendliness. 'You're holding up pretty well under the onslaught of slighted females,' she grinned. 'I'm Doris Maton. I dabbled in public relations before I married into money, I don't think you caught my name in all the fuss.'

'I . . . I'm sorry . . .'

'Don't apologise. I know what it is fending off all our man-hungry sex.' A briskly humorous glance was cast about the room. 'Cats most of them, aren't they?'

Eve had never been anywhere where outspoken comments passed back and forth like everyday chat. 'I . . . think they're just jesting with us newly-weds.' Her own way was to stick to convention.

'Oh sure they are,' she was fixed with a sceptical gleam. There was a look in the tawny eyes which once again, Eve felt, cleaned her out as regards private emotions, but the voice was kindly. 'I like you, Mrs Grantham. I think you'll be good for Ryde. But you have the look of a woman who might break easily under ... er ... excessive pressure.'

'If you mean by that, the kind of jokes I've been hearing here at the reception,' Eve said lightly and untruthfully, 'they don't bother me.'

'Well, I'm glad.' Doris gave her a disbelieving smile. 'If you can handle the snide remarks you're halfway there in our happy little sewing circle. I'm just a wee bit concerned though that you won't have the experience to combat Philippa's particular brand of repartee. That's why I've taken it upon myself—strictly between the two of us of course—to put you on your guard where your husband's former fiancée is concerned.'

Though the news was like a blow to Eve's tottering equilibrium she forced herself to sound amiable and practical as she replied, 'I don't think former fiancées need concern me now, Mrs Maton. If Rydal didn't marry Philippa then obviously it was because he found her unsuitable as a wife.'

'Oh, it wasn't all on his side,' Doris said cryptically. 'They weren't actually engaged. But there was a kind of understanding. Philippa Marchant has titled parents but not a bean to her name, or ever likely to have. As you know, Rydal's sort of lush in that respect ... and that was the understanding,' the woman put in with a wicked twinkle. 'The trouble with Philippa, she likes to play the part of the dog with two bones. She's been attached for some time to Bruno Massaretti, the young man who's been glued to her all afternoon. He's the son of an Italian oil millionaire and she'll probably do all right with him, but I think she's a little piqued that Ryde didn't give her ... well you know, first refusal. And when Philippa's piqued ... well, my dear, she's been known to mulch girls with sweet personalities *before* eating them for breakfast, and I don't want to see you get hurt.'

At any other time Eve would have found the dry wit of the woman and droll mode of speech amusing, and she felt that Doris was sincere in her concern for her own well-being, but it was hardly the conversation with which to grace a wedding reception—her own—so she replied humorously, 'If I'm to be impaled by Philippa's verbal darts, Mrs Maton, then I'll have to try and adopt the attitude of a pin cushion.'

She heard the woman's gay, unoffended laughter, but the grip on her arm was by contrast stern. 'Take care my dear. Marriage is such a beautiful and holy thing. I don't like to see a couple broken up by spiteful underplay.'

She disappeared into the babble and seconds afterwards Rydal was once again at her side, but a long time later in the thick of the reception with him, one half of her mind was still pre-occupied with Doris Maton's words.

The woman didn't know of course, she thought wretchedly, that there was nothing beautiful or holy about Rydal's marriage to her. He was incensed by what he considered her monumental deceit and being a man ruthless in his judgement his ultimate castigation was to tie her to him so that she would not readily escape his contempt.

But she also felt that she knew him well enough to sense that neither was he a man to let a woman as lovely as Philippa Marchant out of his grasp if he so desired her as a wife. This ice-cool logic did little, however, to ease her own bleak unhappiness. She was weary of all the glamour. Tired of being hypocritically bright at well-wishers' remarks, particularly those of the ravishing young women with their barbed smiles.

This was her punishment for loving Rydal. For loving him and not being able to run from him that night when he had first come to her at the Pension Desirade.

CHAPTER TWELVE

THOUGH outwardly she gave no sign of her heartache—brides were always pale with emotion—the effort of disguising it was becoming too much for her, so in an opportune moment she excused herself and went to the powder-room. A few minutes before the mirror would give her the time she needed to acquire a further veneer of serenity for the rest of the party.

She was despairing at her reflection, the haunted look in her eyes, when the door of the powder-room opened and someone else came in. She made a show of straightening a strand of hair beneath her hat and while doing so saw a vaguely familiar figure reflected in the mirror, standing behind her.

'That's a striking outfit you're wearing, Mrs Grantham,' Philippa said huskily. 'Did it come with your holiday gear from England?'

Eve turned. 'I'd hardly be comfortable strolling around Fort de France dressed like this,' she smiled.

'But you're comfortable now . . . oh, so comfortable.' The implication here was not difficult to divine, the look in the violet eyes rather more subtle. 'If you didn't come out here for the sole purpose of the kill, then we must compare notes on how you made Rydal in three easy lessons, or should I say weeks?'

'You've known him for much longer I believe, Miss . . . Marchant, isn't it?' Eve asked pleasantly.

'You can call me Philippa,' came the drawling reply before the tones turned dulcet in another way. 'Rydal and I are something more than friends as you've probably heard.'

'He appears to have many such close friends.' Eve

couldn't help sounding succinct. 'But if you know him that well you're probably aware that Rydal isn't the kind of man to make himself available for any woman's "kill" as you call it. He is the one who does the slaying in his own time.'

She was speaking in metaphors which were painfully applicable in her own case.

Digesting this Philippa viewed her from beneath curling dark lashes. 'There's something odd about you,' she said in her thoughtful, remote way. 'Your homespun qualities don't belong out here. And why would Rydal marry you after a mere three weeks?'

'Perhaps that is something you should ask him yourself.' Eve had made no move to quit the room but she had the strange feeling that her way would have been blocked if she had tried to leave. She was also aware that they were the only two in the powder-room and was seized with the ridiculous notion that the relevant female eyes at the gathering had seen Philippa's entry as well as her own and preferred to give it a wide berth for the time being.

'I intend to,' the throaty voice was saying. 'I didn't come all the way out to Martinique just to attend his wedding you know. I plan to be his guest for some considerable time.'

'If you're staying on the island for the winter,' Eve was purporting to their own weather back home and also to her role as wife—she had that strength at least, 'then I'm sure Rydal will be glad to see you from time to time.'

Her even comment brought a smile to the sensual coral lips. 'He'll be glad to see me,' they murmured while the curvaceous figure in smooth slim-line suit and dainty high heels was sported as thought to verify this. Then with a kind of insolent respect for Eve's married status she added, 'I've a feeling it's going to be an interesting party season, Mrs Grantham. I'm sure you and I are going to find much to talk about at your beach-side retreat of an evening.'

'As far as I know,' Eve smiled, 'my husband is not a keen party-goer. But if we do entertain then I shall look forward to your company.' Desolate, dispirited and jaded emotionally she had no ammunition other than conventional replies for this woman. Curiously, what was taken for her composure appeared to rattle Philippa. It was she who stepped back to leave the way clear but not without a last sultry salvo. 'You can queen it for now, Mrs Grantham, but don't forget that your husband and I are very old friends and I hardly think a three week adventure with a prosaic tourist is going to change things much.'

'I suppose you could say marriage is an adventure. Keeping it intact may, surprisingly, add to the spice,' Eve said and walked out.

She felt as though she had just been circled by a sleek, over-possessive forest cat. Nevertheless she moved erect among the chattering guests until Rydal spotted her and drew her to him for the benefit of the group he was conversing with. 'Make the most of my sweet wife while you can,' he advised suavely, 'I'll soon be taking her off on the first leg of our honeymoon, to the airport.'

There were cries of protest, also joking dissent from the newsmen. 'Where are you off to, sir?' they asked complainingly. 'You're not going to disappear as thoroughly as you did last time, are you?'

'Why should I want to do that?' he replied affably. 'We have no secrets, have we darling?' To Eve who knew all too well the meaning of the glint in his eyes. 'If you would really like to know gentlemen,' expansively he continued, 'I'm about to take my bride on a complete tour of the West Indies; the whole string of islands if you like, from St Martins off Puerto Rico in the north to Tobago and Trinidad in the south. This will be my wedding gift to her.'

There were groans from the pressmen. 'It will cost us a fortune to follow you on a route like that,' the chorused.

'Of course,' he replied complacently. 'But feel free to tag along if you wish.'

A little later they left the reception to more showering of confetti. In the car Rydal said, 'Your bags are packed. There will be just time to change at the house then we must be on our way again to our nuptial nest.' He had become the iron-hard satirist again.

In her room when they arrived she found a travelling dress of uncrushable linen laid out together with matching cherry-pink accessories. Rydal when she went out was in a linen also, a sand-coloured suit with casual lines and impeccable cut. The staff waved them off on the drive and their departure did not come a moment too soon for Eve. Breaking point would have come in a matter of seconds if she had had to go on playing the shy, pleased bride.

But there was no need to pretend anymore, not with the clamped jaw and wintry eye of the man beside her.

She had wondered vaguely how they would cover all the islands he had mentioned on a single honeymoon trip, but when they arrived at the airport she soon saw the reason for his steely assurance. Her elbow in its familiar grasp he guided her across the tarmac to where a crowd circled the gleaming flying machine. 'It's what we call a Learjet,' Rydal told her. 'It's not enough to build aeroplanes, you have to know how to fly them.'

The blue and silver private jet had a bullet-shaped nose, wide wind-screened pilot's cabin and port-holes along the sides. As Rydal handed her towards the stairway they were crushed by more well-wishers and newsmen. His wide shoulders provided ample protection for her while he quipped with the eager spectators.

At the top of the stairway he thrust her inside and stood a moment until airport officials cleared the area.

From within the aircraft Eve had a framed view of Rydal in the hatchway. She alone knew the reason for the grey tinge behind his smile, the drawn look of his profile as an airfield gust tossed his hair. He was an angry man. But why did she feel, looking at him now, that he was also a broken one?

She waved to the receding people because she felt it was expected of her, then turned inside. The interior of the jet was fitted out like a carpeted lounge. There were armchairs, coffee table, drinks cabinet, every luxury in overall tones of claret and cream. When Rydal came in and closed the hatch door she felt a terrible, yet delectable intimacy in the low-roofed interior.

'Come on up front.' Now that they were alone his grasp on her was almost savage. 'You wanted to know all about my aircraft activities. Well now you're going to find out.' He strapped her in the seat beside him then took over at the controls. He no longer smiled. She never would have thought she would miss that ice-cold sneer, but she felt now that it was preferable to the deadly gravity on his face.

She could hear faint voices on his earphones and saw him perform functions with the battery of dials in front of him. His taxi-ing and eventual departure from the runway was smooth she felt. Though she knew little about flying in any form herself, his icy precision and keen flint-eyed judgement was something that even she was made aware of.

It was only when they took to the skies that that dreadful smile returned to his lips, though he appeared as grimly cool as ever at the controls. 'Let's take a look at Martinique shall we?' he said. 'Before we bid it farewell.'

When the nose dived abruptly a horror rose in Eve's throat. Within seconds of roaring upwards they were plunging towards the sea. When they appeared to be only inches above it they straightened out and she saw the land whipping away beneath them. 'This is what we call "skin-flying",' Rydel told her conversationally. 'Unfortunately it doesn't give a lot of time to view one's favourite spots. You know, like the Guamel's plantation in our case, and the cliff nook above the fishing village of Marimant. Oh and we mustn't forget that cosy session we had on the bluff at Mount Pelee. But I'm sure you're more likely to appreciate this first hand insight into the rudimentary elements of my career in the aircraft business.'

His heavy sarcasm cut deeper even than her rigid fear as coconut palms, blazing blossom and cultivated fields appeared to brush the base of her seat in passing. They would soar just in time when a tree-clad mountain came terrifyingly close to blotting out the light, and blue coves, toy-town villages and thick forests wheeled past her eyes, a dizzying blur made more sickening by the constant banking and rolling of their stealthily thundering conveyance.

'That's Martinique that was!' The gratingly amused voice came to her ears while she was trying to adjust to the sight of green-blue sea flashing by beneath her. His jokes were as macabre as his sense of humour.

Flying on an even keel was bliss after what she had been through, and as they began to climb she struggled up from an overpowering nausea only to hear him exclaim chattily, 'Now where shall we start? I know! The Virgin Islands are only a short way from here as the crow flies—or as our Learjet spins along,' he grinned. 'Let's give them a whirl shall we?'

They rode through the blue heavens for little more than twenty minutes then Eve felt her heart in her throat again as they plunged towards the sprinkling of green specks in the ocean with the speed of a plummeting meteor.

'There you are,' she was told drily from the pilot's seat as white beaches, fishing harbours and waving palm fronds almost came into the cabin before spinning away to leave translucent sea. 'Take your pick. There's Beef Island, Salt Island, Ginger Island, Prickly Pear Island . . . But from a flying point of view you could say that if I'd designed this thing we're travelling in, and it had to be tested for safety, then this would be a good way to look for wing stress and such things . . .'

Nothing was said about the stress of the occupants and Eve fought to remain upright in her seat while every nerve in her body cried out for clemency. She did not know how long she could keep from blacking out. She looked like a ghost, she knew it. A chalk-white damp-browed wraith of herself, tormented by flashing land fragments and more malignant uprushes of turquoise ocean. She became suspended in an unmitigated fear so that time ceased to exist, but it seemed an age later when the world righted itself and they were cruising towards a burnished gold sunset dripping liquid copper on the clouds and highlighting the infinite blue of the stratosphere.

'Well, I hope you enjoyed your lesson on aeronautics, Mrs Grantham.' Those taunting inflections again. 'I'm sure you're a little wiser now as to what makes me tick.'

The afternoon had been full of shocks, but the greatest of all was when she turned her gaze, for the first time since starting out, to his. The sneer was there, that awful slash of humour, the exhilaration of hate also, but his face was grey beneath it all, that putty grey which made his features appear raw-boned. And there was a wound in his eyes that no smile of contempt could entirely erase.

Eve was shocked to the root of her being in a way which had nothing to do with flight nerves; shocked and trembling and a little starry-eyed in her heart. Had he loved her as she loved him? Had his wild aerobatics of the past hour or so, been a way of punishing not only her, but himself for being fool enough—or so he thought—to believe that she had been genuine in her companionableness? A way of giving vent to a hurt that, man as he was, he would never admit to?

Her mind, rose-lit and dazzled, careered back to their outings together, to the times when he had held her hand, not always over rough ground; to when he had assisted her across some obstacle and kept his arm longer than necessary around her waist. Had her heart been right in hoarding these simple gestures like a greedy squirrel stores nuts, to nurture her love? It pounded now with both excitement and melancholy. She could think of nothing else so that Rydal's telling her, 'We'll start our honeymoon on St Martins,' and their gradual descent, took place in a silvery mist not without its shadows behind her eyes, as did their disembarking from the jet later to a waiting car in the violet dusk and their ride through tropical vegetation to a house by the sea.

It was a lovely setting which hurt her already bruised heart by its beauty. The house, of island design, but with a luxury aura, stood almost on the ivory beach, its windows and verandas softly lit, casting a glow over the deserted shell-strewn stretches, and gently lapping night-smooth Caribbean.

Coloured staff came out to carry in their luggage. 'It's handy to have friends you can rely on,' Rydal said, helping her from the car. 'We've got the use of the servants till we've eaten then they'll disappear. Thoughtful of them, isn't it?'

Eve swayed in the darkness. His nearness in the blossom-scented evening caused her unbearable sweetness and pain. Must he always make her aware of his contempt? Did everything he said to her have to contain hidden barbs?

The bungalow was as attractive inside as out. The furnishings and decor of the large living room were dominantly of polished bamboo and gay chintz, but blended in such a way as to give both comfort and style. A semi-screened section showed a similarly bamboo charm dining area where a long table was impressively laid out for two with flowers, fruit and elegant tableware.

They were shown to where they could freshen up after their journey. The bedroom suite was almost as large as the living room. The decor here was cool white and gold, and french windows opened on to a veranda directly overlooking the starlit ocean.

Eve was thankful for the subdued lighting at the dining table. She was still feeling the after-effects of the cruel torment she had suffered at Rydal's hands, and her waxen features were not something she could disguise despite her deadened, yet composed, air. The meal would have been perfect—she gripped her fork with the anguish of it—for a newly wedded ecstatically happy pair. It was island cooking at its best, with courses typical, she supposed, of French St Martins. But the food might have been sawdust as far as she was concerned, even though the husband who despised her made every effort to project an air of light-heartedness at the table.

As he had said would happen, once the meal was over and the remains cleared, the house fell silent. Leaving the soft glow of the living room she went out on to the veranda and stood listening to the night. She longed to enfold herself in the starlit peace but memories, dear to her now in retrospect, made this impossible.

She thought of that very first afternoon when Rydal had lifted her into his arms out of reach of the guard dogs on his beach. She would far rather have his wrath of that day than the anger which consumed him now. And to have his arms about her even impersonally would ease a little her desperate need for him.

In the distance she could hear the faint steel drum sound of the islands. There was something poignant about the music in her present mood. How, she wondered, would she be feeling right now if she had successfully escaped Rydal that night at Corobrier and returned to Ingledene without running into him again? Could she honestly say she would have preferred that existence to the one she had now? No! She cried out wordlessly to the night. To be here with him was worth all the pangs and torment of his bitterness.

She became aware of a movement nearby. Rydal was in the shadows in silk dressing gown. 'I think it's time we turned in don't you, Mrs Grantham?' The heavy satire was there. 'You'll probably want to shower away the dust of travel. I've laid your nightwear out in a nice handy place.'

Feeling deathly cold Eve preceded him indoors. She bathed and mechanically perfumed her body. If she had ever had dreams about her wedding night she could hardly have envisaged a situation like this.

She donned the gossamer lace-trimmed nightdress. Its pale coffee colour heightened her waxen features and gave her an ethereal quality. She moved into the bedroom, statuesque and a little remote.

Rydal was beside the open french windows. 'Come and look at the view my dear,' he invited with a thin smile. 'We shouldn't let all this beauty go by the board even though this is our honeymoon night.'

Eve did as he asked. She had already experienced the magic under the stars but they were like lanterns now over the sea, unless it was Rydal's overpowering nearness which blurred her vision and her senses. She melted at the sight of palms in silhouette, at the scent of oleander beyond the veranda, but it was the breathless proximity of the man who was now her husband which caused the sweet havoc inside her.

Her back to him he drew her against him so that his

lips brushed her hair, but his voice was silky and over-smooth as he murmured, 'Isn't this a cosy wedding night? I hope you've got your book and pencil at the ready to describe in detail how the designing genius Rydal Grantham performs in the marriage chamber.'

Eve was cut to the deepest regions of her love by the remark. He must have sensed her woodenness for he swung her to face him and said with a savage smile, 'You'll admit I'm entitled to extract vengeance in any way I like for your double-dealing tourist act.'

'I'm your wife,' she acknowledged sadly.

'That's right, my wife and my bed-mate.' He brought his head down and kissed her long and brutally. Every nuance of his embrace indicated his steely distaste, but there was something else powerfully aflame amidst the ungentleness of his anger and to Eve, knowing at last his lips on hers, it was like the tender linking of souls in a wash of icy disillusionment on the one side and bleak unhappiness on the other.

'Well, what are we waiting for?' He had lifted his head, his eyes glinting perhaps to disguise the tumult there. 'You're looking every inch the wife tonight—not a trace of printers ink—let's see how learning about your subject at first hand has improved your style.'

He swung her up in his arms as though she were a mere rag doll, and her limpness at first resembled one. But then as he moved towards the bed she was reminded of that salty gossip Doris Maton's words 'marriage is such a beautiful and holy thing' and she knew that she would not besmirch her side of it with desire wearing the cloak of love.

She wanted this man as a husband but not before she had cleared herself in his eyes. 'Rydal, please! Wait! I want to talk to you.' Hitting the satin coverlet she looked up desperately into his face. His features dark he raised himself inches from her lips. He eyed her bemusedly, searching her drained countenance with his gaze while his mouth twisted as he spoke. 'What's this? Are we to have the confessions of a news scribe—or would that be scribess?—at this untimely moment?'

'Will you believe me when I tell you there was never any book and pencil—or association with printers ink?' Her breathing was rapid.

'Oh, I see!' he smiled unpleasantly. 'You've decided to conduct your own defence. Well you've picked a rum time for it, Mrs Grantham, and lying is hardly likely to improve relations between us bedfellows, so to speak.'

'I'm not lying,' she quivered. 'I wouldn't know how to report on a village jumble sale let alone cover the movements of the internationally famous, like yourself.'

From where he leaned a little above her he gave her a mocking bow. His gaze narrowing he commented, 'Still pushing the old rustic image. I'll admit you wear it well but it doesn't fool me anymore. Behind those sylvan soft eyes of yours is a snapshot brain highly trained to pay sharp attention to detail.'

She smiled with both impatience and scorn. 'Why do you say that? Because I stumbled on your beach one day and aroused your guard dogs?'

'Stumbled! With the very able assistance of that brother of yours.'

'All right, he did help me over the rocks,' she confessed. 'But don't you see! I had no idea what he was planning. I went on that beach believing it to be a deserted spot. He didn't tell me it was owned by someone he particularly wanted to interview.'

'Yet you played the quaking damsel to the T, even dropping prettily in a dead faint at my feet with one eye open to catch what was going on, of course.'

'I was shocked at the savagery of your animals,' she retorted. 'It was you who presumed I was incapable of rising. You who transported me off before I could speak.'

For a second his gaze was far distant as though he

too was re-living those moments when he had gathered her into his arms. In the blue depths of his eyes there might have been a softening at remembering but all too soon it turned to cynicism as he drawled, 'Lucky for you. It got you the introduction you were angling for, though I must have seemed a tough nut to crack, you lying there all defenceless on my divan and everything.'

They said that love and hate went hand in hand, and Eve felt some of the latter rising up in her now at his nasty implication. 'Just like all people who figure in the news,' she scoffed, 'you're beginning to believe your own publicity. Not even to get to meet *you* would I have knowingly braved those slobbering Doberman Pinchers. I'm telling you it was Rex's idea and he didn't breathe a word of his plan to me.'

'Of course he didn't. And naturally it was pure coincidence that of all the dozens of villages on the island you had to be in Corobrier, well off the beaten track for the average sightseer, on the same night I was, a couple of days later.'

'All right,' she said tremulously, 'I'll admit that I went there to please Rex. I'll admit that I let him talk me into faking an accidental meeting with you a second time, with a view to striking up a friendship. But I lost my nerve at the last minute. I was running away when——'

'When you *accidentally* ran into me. Such timing can only be described as phenomenal, Mrs Grantham. I bet brother Rex was pleased.' His smile supercilious he rested on one arm above her. 'What puzzles me is, why this spirited attempt now to whitewash your actions? Why the second thoughts on your shot-gun bridal state? Could it be that you're finding your present role as my wife, waited on by servants, flown around by private jet—albeit a little bumpy,' he grinned sadistically, 'a lot cushier than snooping out profile sketches for brother Rex?'

Oh he could be a beast! A cold, inhuman beast! He

may be angry but it was nothing to the seething fury she felt now. How dare he foul her love for him with talk of material gain? She would want him if they were both destined to live the rest of their lives in a cave! She wanted to weep at the shattering of something sacred but instead she lashed out with her hand hoping to wipe off some of that sickeningly superior sarcasm on his face.

She might have known that it would be a puny effort compared to his strength. She had no resistance in her, he had seen to that with his deadly jet antics over the islands. He grabbed her wrist before it came anywhere near making satisfying contact and breathlessly in his grip she could only gasp out, eyes flashing, 'The trouble with you is that you can't see beyond the Philippa Marchants of this world. Not everybody's after your money. Least of all me.'

His look was expressive. 'Philippa's a fortune hunter, but she doesn't pretend to be anything else. I appreciate that.'

'May you long remain good friends,' Eve glowered.

'I expect we shall,' he said with a nonchalance which had her writhing again.

'If I dealt in profile sketches as you call it,' she spat, 'I wouldn't forget to paint in that fidelity to your wife is not likely to be one of your strong points in marriage.'

'Right again, no doubt, but don't forget the wife is expected to take it all lying down in the bridal bed.' His smile was laconic but his eyes blazed and Eve could see that she had got nowhere with her frantic explanations. She had tried to make him see that there had been no ulterior motive behind her friendship with him and only succeeded in losing her temper; a rare happening for her.

Nothing had changed between them except she had made the mistake of baiting him with her flare-up. He was a man pushed to the brink with his emotions and as he gazed down at her pinioned by his strength, his eyes darkened to a frightening glowing intensity. She waited for his mouth to descend brutally on hers, something dying in her that it couldn't have been different. Then he raised himself and said thickly, 'Get out of my sight before I forget I'm your husband, not a rapist.'

Her eyes bright with tears Eve dragged herself away and left the room snatching up a negligée in passing. She went through and out on to the living room veranda where the tears provided some relief for her desperate unhappiness. Rydal was a ruthless, merciless tyrant of a man when crossed, but any woman who could capture his love would be cherished and protected by him till the end of his days.

She sank into a chair and dropped her face in her hands. What was the use of yearning for what might have been? He didn't believe her and there was no way she could make him believe her. She was as lost in her love for him as a spirit in the wilderness. But how was it that in that same wilderness as she tried to warm herself with dreams, a shape dear to her hovered then loomed close? Was the feel of strong arms about her, scooping her from the chair where she had curled in sleep the product of her affection-starved imagination; the passage through dimly lit rooms and the eventual caress of satin coverlets against her skin?

When she awoke in the morning in the huge silken bed she knew that those moments last night had had nothing to do with her fantasising heart. But then she saw the pillow next to hers, smooth and undented, and the wilderness too became a bleak reality.

CHAPTER THIRTEEN

THEY spent several days in St Martin, an island seemingly content to slumber languidly in the sun. Women with broad smiles sat on little stools in the market place selling breadfruit and cinnamon. Fishermen chugged home in the evening with their catch, to a clamorous welcome.

At the smart hotels outside Philipsburg the capital, Eve met various acquaintances of Rydal's; sun-seekers who threw private parties and took midnight dips in the swimming pool. The men were charming towards her, the women smilingly distant. They found it hard to forgive her for carrying off the trophy of the season. Knowing this Eve would smile bitterly to herself. She had to suffer Rydal's double-edged way of purporting to be the ideal husband, one half of him projecting an attentive air, the other, known only to the two of them, exuding his disdain.

Thankfully he kept the house on the beach inviolate of visitors. During the day they were fed and pampered by the servants. At night time they were left alone. Alone with the heart-breakingly beautiful sunsets, the velvet warm darkness, and their separate rooms.

They jetted down the string of Caribbean islands in this way. To Guadeloupe for Christmas with its stately Creole style plantation homes of wood and stone recalling the old days of sugar prosperity; St Lucia a jewel of rugged green jungle and dazzling beaches; St Vincent the home of coconuts, cacao, eddoes and yams.

On Tobago, Eve would stand on the veranda of their hill house of an evening and listen to the music drifting up from the beach-side hotels. Without fail the tune that had haunted her most on this trip would come to her on the breeze and she would grip the veranda rails to keep the tears from her eyes. She couldn't hear the words being sung but she didn't need to, they were engraved on her heart, a mocking epitaph to her loneliness.

> *'I'm with you once more under the stars*
> *And down by the shore an orchestra's playing*
> *Even the palms seem to be swaying*
> *When they begin the beguine . . .'*

How many times had she cried out inside while dining out, *Please don't let them begin the beguine*. But they always did. It was the song of the islands. And she was compelled to dance with Rydal, to have him hold her close, so close she could almost imagine they were back on the Pointe du Bout hotel dance floor in Martinique after their ferry ride across the bay . . . But it was only the words of the song lulling her into a false sense of rapture. Rydal despised her and he had chained her to him in marriage as penance.

They danced and dined and partied their way on a honeymoon course, the gauntlet she had to run through Rydal's beautiful female admirers—where on earth did he dig her up? She could almost hear them saying behind their vanquished smiles—far less of a torment than the tune which she would always associate with the happiest night of her life.

But one evening in Trinidad she found herself dancing the beguine with someone other than her husband.

Trinidad with its lush scenery, multi-racial population and imposing colonial palaces in its capital, Port of Spain. The Granthams had a house set in teak, nutmeg and wild cotton silk trees overlooking the city. They began breakfast each day with a choice of fresh tropical juices and fruits, orange paw-paws, pineapple, mangoes and water-melon. The view from the veranda of sparkling blue harbour, cruise ships and misted-over town dwellings was surpassed only by the night-time view of twinkling coastline and jewelled city lights.

They went by car, Rydal at the wheel, to the beach-side nightspots outside town. Music swelled up in the islands at this hour. There was dancing in the dark, in the moonlight and in the streets. Most of the night-life however centred round the hotels, the entertainment varying from Calypso to fire-eaters. But there was always a British contingent that Rydal knew of, either enjoying the nightclub amenities or in an adjoining beach-side residence.

Early on in their stay Eve met John and Paula Blakeley, a wealthy middle-aged couple who came out to Trinidad for two months every year to keep an eye on their estate. John, bearded and greying, travelled the world buying and selling antiques. Paula, slightly bored with the arrangement, had cottoned on to making zircon replicas of priceless jewellery owned by her husband's clientele. The idea was that zircons, looking exactly like diamonds, but nowhere near as valuable, provided contented minds for the wearer while the family heirlooms remained safely in the bank vaults.

The Blakeleys, a warm-hearted pair, unaffected by their success, were typical of many of Rydal's friends with properties on the islands whom Eve had met on their travels.

She took to them at once. Their rambling bungalow was part of several acres of coconut-palm land and possessed its own private beach. A warm, tropical sea at its door, graceful palms growing down to the rear lawn it was the ideal setting for dinner-parties and gatherings. And as the antique specialist was a long-standing friend of Rydal's, the Granthams were regular visitors to the Blakeley's household.

Paula had a gift for entertaining and a couple of

dozen people using her domain as their own caused her no flurry at all. She had an excellent house-staff. The after-dinner amusements, however, she arranged herself. She couldn't know of course that the old Cole Porter classic, among her taped music for dancing, caused one of her guests an acute stab of nostalgia every time it was played. Or how much it cost Eve to appear blithely disinterested in the song when someone in the gathering asked her to dance.

That was how she came to know Peter Arnwood. He was tall, bronze-haired with a mature width of shoulder and a very nice smile. Having met him already at the dinner table Eve danced with him mechanically. Rydal was deep in conversation with John Blakeley at the bar, but partners were chosen at random regardless of married status as at all good parties and there was nothing to be done but oblige gracefully.

She was wearing a gown of soft aquamarine material trimmed with chiffon. Her hair was dressed regularly and she had learned to take this new groomed image of herself in her stride. It sometimes, however, caused covert interest among the male members of a gathering as it appeared to be doing now.

'How does it feel to be the brand new wife of a leading wizard in the aircraft world?' she was asked on the dance space.

'The same as it would being married to any man of one's choice, I suppose,' she replied guilelessly.

'But not any man could afford to give his wife a personally piloted jet trip around the entire Caribbean as a wedding gift.'

Eve's dance steps remained smooth. Her partner was well informed.

'You could say it's a question of relativity,' she was deliberately facetious. 'Many a woman has been just as thrilled with a trip round Brighton pier. I don't think it matters too much if the honeymoon is a happy one.'

'And is your honeymoon a happy one?'

Eve did fluff a step then. No one had ever asked her that before. Perhaps there had been no need to. Despite her abysmal unhappiness her love for Rydal must have shone out of her in some ways making it detectable to the discerning eye. But this man appeared to have a shrewder brand of vision. He had asked the question not in a probing or offensive way but simply matter-of-fact frankness.

She countered the query by enquiring, 'Are you married, Mr Arnwood?'

'Please, call me Peter,' he beseeched smiling. And in reply to her question, 'No, I'm not married, Mrs Grantham . . . or may I call you Eve?'

She left this open and not knowing quite what to say next resorted to amusement. 'Well, it's no good me asking you your definition of a happy honeymoon. Maybe we should meet in a few years time when you're better equipped to compare notes.'

'I hope we'll see each other again before that,' he said, his merry hazel eyes attractively imploring.

Once again Eve demurred to make comment. The tune had long since changed and they were now dancing a disco number which required very little movement over the space. 'What do you think of Trinidad?' Peter asked conversationally while he moved his body in a very polished style of rhythm.

'What would anyone think of Trinidad?' she smiled reminiscently. 'Spice-scented, tropical and romantic.'

In an unwise and unguarded moment, speaking her thoughts aloud she was pierced by an exquisite misery. Recovering herself almost at once she back-handed the question by saying, 'What do you know about the island?'

The amber gaze seemed to miss nothing of the waxen paleness which had momentarily robbed her of her serenity.

'A fair amount,' he grinned. 'My favourite spot is the Blue Basin near Diego Martin valley. Have you toured that way?'

'We've been with John and Paula and other friends to most of the beauty spots locally,' Eve nodded.

A coppery eyebrow lifted crookedly. 'This hibiscus-edged pool fed by a waterfall is not meant to be enjoyed in a group. A couple can swim there like Tarzan and Jane.'

Though it was tempting to the point of bringing a lump to her throat she didn't permit herself the bliss of imagining Rydal and herself behaving with such carefree abandon. Instead she teased out loud, 'And what other jewel-like locations on the island can you quote on with such authority?'

In much the same vein he glanced round them at the party atmosphere and noise and complained twink-lingly, 'This is no place to expound. Let's go somewhere where we can hear ourselves talk.'

There was an open doorway nearby and finding herself being eased towards it Eve decided that a little fresh air might soothe her throbbing temples. But the strain of disguising her desolation left her totally unprepared for the utter peace and loveliness of the outside.

The stars glowed in the black roof of the world with sequin clarity, through the palms a segment of moon rode drifting silvered clouds. Eve's heart swelled and in its leadenness it ached too, in the vast silence, with a desperate loneliness. Nights like this were made to share. Above the whisper of waves she could hear the familiar cadence which almost broke her will to keep a dry eye.

She was reminded that she was not alone when a voice said, 'All of a sudden you're not interested in my scenic knowledge.'

With a slight start she forced a smile at the dry tones.

'I'm sorry, I was listening to the music coming from beyond the trees.'

Peter Arnwood inclined an ear. 'That's the first time I've seen a fellow Anglo-Saxon go to pieces over a steel-band sound.' In the shadows she felt that his gaze remained with her. Still listening she tried to sound detached. 'It does have a certain haunting quality when heard from a distance.'

He was standing quite near to her. 'You're a sensitive woman, Eve,' he said. 'You feel things deeply. It may surprise you to know that I get pretty cut up myself when I'm confronted with something like this.' Quietly he glanced around him at the trembling frangipani, silvered waves and looming palms. 'These islands for you and me and all those like us,' with a nod he indicated the indoors, 'are not just exotic and more colourful from what we know back home. There's some kind of mystic difference here. I feel it and I'm often moved by it.'

Eve was not keen to investigate such a mood. 'All islands are supposed to have a magic,' she said lightly. 'Maybe it's just that. The difference between a marooned scrap of earth and a land mass.'

'Could be,' he shrugged. 'But I sense something at sunset when the scarlet ibis fills the sky with clouds of flame, and on nights like this.' He studied the distant stars with his gaze.

'And where would one see scarlet ibis?' Eve asked not without interest. 'Not over the city I'm sure.'

'Nope,' he grinned, his mood lightening. 'You have to go to the Caroni bird sanctuary about seven miles south of Port of Spain. It's an excursion by boat, very pleasant, along the Wayama river past endless mangrove trees. All kinds of birds nest in the sanctuary. It's quite a sight. If you're interested I can book you a trip.'

'You wouldn't be connected with a tour operator,

would you?' She gave him a sideways smile.

'No. Just keen for you to make the most of your stay in Trinidad.'

At the grave tones she was compelled to say flippantly, 'What makes you think I'm not doing just that?'

'I told you Eve. I'm sensitive too.'

Something in his manner made her pretend to peer at her wrist watch. 'It ... must be getting late. The party will be finishing soon. I'd better go and find my husband.'

'Eve ...' he put a restraining hand on her arm, 'if you must rush away. Thanks for the dance ... and the chat.' She left with Rydal soon after.

She didn't know how it came about but Peter Arnwood turned up at every gathering they attended during their stay in Trinidad. He had said nothing to Eve of his background but she assumed he was sufficiently familiar with the British community on the island to get invited out so often.

He made a point of partnering Eve at least once during the evening if there was dancing. And sometimes when Rydal was engrossed elsewhere he would propel her to some corner with a drink and lift her out of herself with his engaging conversation. He was a man full of warmth, and knowing only Rydal's cynical disdain when they were alone, Eve's starved heart was pathetically eager to unfurl itself in the glow of his friendship, even though she played the part unfailingly of the contented honeymoon wife. He was an amusing companion besides being a deeply sincere one.

Whenever they met they talked about home and travel and sights to be seen on the island. Then one evening while they were on the subject of out of town diversions he suggested taking her to the Caroni bird sanctuary.

Eve was old-fashioned enough to appear shocked. 'I

couldn't do that, Peter,' she said over the top of her drink. 'I'm a married woman you know.'

'I mean as a friend.' He smiled at her misgivings, and looking around, 'I'll ask your husband if you like?'

Whether he would have done Eve wasn't sure but she quickly put a hand on his sleeve. 'No, don't do that . . . Rydal's playing golf tomorrow afternoon with John Blakeley. I . . . could go to the bird sanctuary then, I suppose . . .'

'Wonderful, Eve! You'll enjoy it I promise you,' he said gently. 'Where shall I pick you up?'

'You could come to the house,' Eve decided as they had nothing to hide. 'We're on the Carados hill road. Lucetta is a lofty residence standing in its own . . .'

'I know the place. I'll be there about three,' Peter nodded reaching for more drinks from a passing tray. His back to her momentarily, Eve was mildly surprised that he was familiar with the whereabouts of their honeymoon residence, but then he had shown himself to be well-informed on most things concerning the island.

She was sitting on the veranda flicking through a magazine the next afternoon when Rydal drove off for his golf date. She rose as soon as he had gone and went indoors to collect her handbag. She had a few minutes to spare and could have walked down the hill some way to meet Peter, but that would have appeared clandestine. She preferred to wait until he drove up to the house in full view of the servants.

It was a little after three when he arrived. His bronze-gold hair gleamed in the sun in his open-topped car. He wore sports shirt and slacks and looked smilingly relaxed. Eve joined him, taking her time from the veranda down to the drive. She had put on an expensively simple sun-dress and carried a matching bolero in case it was cool on the river ride.

The sanctuary was all that Peter claimed it to be. From

the boat Eve saw tiny crabs and oysters in the tangle of long roots of the mangrove trees. Magnificent blue and white heron skimmed the waters surface or stood like Dresden china replicas against the lowering sun. And when all the birds and the scarlet ibis settled at last on the mangroves, the trees were transformed as though heavy with Christmas decoration.

Returning to town Peter didn't drive straight up to the hill house as she had expected. He stopped some way from the wooded residence at a curve on the roadside where Port of Spain, the city, lay spread below them. It was a little used route and they had the area to themselves as they stood beside a low wall and watched dusk settle over the bay and buildings.

Gazing at the twilight scene Eve felt the desolation burgeoning within her as it always did at this hour.

His eyes on her rather than the view Peter said, 'A penny for your thoughts. Wasn't the afternoon to your liking?'

'You know it was,' she turned to him. 'I've enjoyed it immensely, Peter. And thank you for being kind enough to take me.'

'My pleasure,' he bowed a little ironically. 'I'd show you the president's private palace if I thought it would put a shine in those lovely, bleak eyes of yours.'

Eve turned back again to the view. Sometimes she felt that Peter was a little too discerning. 'I know I'm on my honeymoon,' she said with forced gaiety, 'but it's rather old hat don't you think, to go around permanently starry-eyed?'

'I don't think there's anything old hat in showing you're in love,' he replied slowly. 'After all that's what marriage is all about isn't it?'

'Your views are outdated, Peter,' she managed a laugh. 'Nowadays nobody gets excited about legalising a partnership. It's just routine in many cases.'

'But not in yours.' Gently he turned her towards him.

'Don't try to hide it from me, Eve.' His gaze was deeply searching. 'I've known for some time that you're not happy.'

With such gravity of speech there wasn't much she could do to deny it. All of a sudden, knowing this man's nearness, his warmth, his eagerness to assist where he could, it was tempting to open the floodgates of her despair. 'Oh, Peter.' She blinked back the tears quiveringly. 'There's nothing you can do I'm afraid.'

'I can listen to your troubles.' His hands on her shoulders, they gripped her with peculiar intensity. 'Why are you so unhappy, Eve? You know you can tell me.'

'Please,' she turned her head. 'I'd rather not talk about it.'

'All right.' He dropped his hands. 'Well, can we keep up the outings? I'm not exactly the world's greatest cheerleader, but I think I helped a bit this afternoon. I'd like to go on helping if I may.'

'Of course.' She smiled wanly. 'I'd better go now. I can walk the rest of the way. And, Peter,' she turned back to give him a grateful look. 'Thank you for being a good friend.'

'I'm always here when you want me,' he smiled gravely beside the car. And with a wave, 'I'll give you a ring tomorrow.'

It wasn't difficult spending a few hours away from the house every now and then. Rydal would tell her his plans for the afternoon. Sometimes he would expect her to accompany him. But there were occasions when it was a fishing trip or some such masculine pursuit, and she would be free to amuse herself as she wished. She found Peter's companionship a balm to her leaden spirits. She would often marvel to herself that she had been fortunate enough to run into him on an island not overpopulated with their own kind.

He never referred to her marriage with Rydal until

one afternoon when they were finishing a fruit punch at a cafe bar in town. During a lull in their conversation which had been for the most part desultory, on Eve's part, he enquired gently, 'Do you feel now that you can trust me enough to tell me what's troubling you?'

'It wouldn't help,' she smiled.

'It might.' He looked deep into her eyes. 'Talking does a lot to ease the strain and I know you're going through a hell of some kind.'

It was her private hell she wanted to say, but Peter's concern made this sort of reply difficult. Dear Peter. He had been so kind. Would it matter if she told him the whole story? All at once the idea of giving vent to her secret misery appealed to her heavy heart. Perhaps he was right. Perhaps talk with someone, and especially Peter, would help her to recover her fast disintegrating self-control.

Still, she demurred by saying, 'You wouldn't want to listen to what amounts to no more than a domestic tiff.'

'Who said I wouldn't want to listen?' He was emphatic in his reply. 'That's what friends are for aren't they?' He glanced at his watch. 'You'll have to be getting back. But I'll come to the house one day.'

'To Lucetta?' Eve looked a little uncertain.

'It'll be okay,' he smiled leading her to his car. 'I'll give you a ring first. We're going to have that talk, Eve.'

He did give her a ring, one morning. A servant came to tell her that a Mr Arnwood wished to speak to her. She took the call in the hall. 'Hello, Eve.' It was the warm friendly voice that she knew so well. 'I'll be up this afternoon about three. Will you be in?'

'Well ... yes, I think so ... but ...'

'Good. I'll be along then.'

'Peter ...' Before she could voice her misgivings he had rung off. She was replacing the receiver uncertainly when Rydal strode into the hall. 'Ah there you are!' He looked at the phone and at her momentarily before saying, 'I'm off for a game of polo this afternoon. One or two of the wives are joining the party as spectators. Would you care to come along?'

'I ... don't think so.' Eve was experiencing mild relief. How lucky that Peter had chosen a day when Rydal was going out.

'What, you don't want to come and watch your husband shine at his favourite sport?' The tones were heavily satirical, his gaze on her keen and somehow mockingly probing.

'I ... I've got one or two bits to do.' She felt it was a lame excuse, but he appeared to accept it.

'Very well, if that's your choice,' he said with a curled smile and drifted off.

He drove away for his polo game at two-thirty. Eve watched him go then went to her room to prepare for Peter's visit. She hated the feeling of being clandestine. After all the man was just a good friend. And of course the fact that he was coming to the house in full view of the servants showed that she had nothing to hide.

He drove up a little before three. Eve was glad to see him because for some reason now the waiting had made her tense. She couldn't bring herself to invite him indoors, but had drinks brought out on to the veranda where the magnificent view induced a relaxed air. There were comfortable basketwork armchairs to recline in but Peter chose the matching cushioned settee. 'Let's sit here shall we?' He patted the seat beside him. 'I want to make it as easy as I can for you to tell me your troubles.'

'You're good to me, Peter,' she sighed and took the seat next to him. 'I don't know why you waste your time with me when there's so much fun to be had on the island.'

'I'm doing what I want to do, being here beside you,' he smiled. 'Now, how about us getting down to the subject of those sad eyes?'

She shrugged, all at once reticent to bare her heart, even to Peter. 'I don't know where to start,' she laughed awkwardly.

'Well, to use an old cliché,' he put a hand in his pocket, 'why not try at the beginning?' She had thought he had meant to bring out cigarettes, but perhaps he had changed his mind.

She swallowed. 'That would be when I first came out to Martinique on holiday.'

'And when did you meet Rydal?' Peter prompted her. He leaned forwards as though to give all his attention to what she said.

'Oh . . . in rather odd circumstances.' There was a far-away look in her eyes. It was strange how nothing she had been through since had dulled the overpowering clarity of that first day on the beach. She was wondering how she could put this into words when a footstep sounded in the doorway from inside the house. She half-turned her glance expecting to see a servant there and was riveted to find that it was Rydal's big frame filling the entrance.

'Ah, good afternoon.' He strolled out on to the veranda without any signs of sporting equipment in tow. 'I see you have a visitor, Eve. Pete isn't it? Pete Arnwood?'

The two of them were staring up slightly open-mouthed. 'Ah, yes! The polo match.' He seemed aware of their dilemma. 'Well I did actually start out, but then I had an attack of conscience. I thought, if my wife didn't want to accompany me then perhaps it was my place as a honeymoon husband to remain at her side.' Because there was only a strained silence he went on, 'Well, don't let me interrupt anything. If you two are occupied I can always read a paper or something.'

'Some other time perhaps,' Peter had got to his feet. Eve had never seen him look so cold. And was that discomfort in his smile?

'What going so soon, Pete!' Rydal said matily. 'Can't I invite you to a man-to-man drink?'

His sarcasm was ignored as Eve was told, 'We'll leave things as they are for now, Mrs Grantham. I'll see you around.'

'Well if you must go.' The sardonic tones again. 'Make sure you take everything with you.' In one quick stride Rydal was at Peter's side to tap his pocket. 'Ah yes. I see you're intact. But don't forget to switch off old man. A waste of good tape.'

Befogged Eve watched Peter move off with a wooden expression. He disappeared down the veranda steps and seconds later she heard his car slewing out of the gates towards town.

'Well, it seems I'm not the most popular host hereabouts,' Rydal mused laconically at the cloud of dust along the road.

'I ... I don't understand,' Eve said a little angrily. 'Peter is a friend of mine. Why were you so rude to him?'

'I? Rude?' The blue eyes now burned with mockery. 'My dear, you saw for yourself, I made every attempt to be chummy.'

'You were horrid to him,' she retorted. 'And what was all that business about his pocket. How could you?'

'I could,' he shrugged simply, 'because your news-paper-man friend was just about to tape an interview with you on the recorder in his pocket.'

'My newspaper-man fr . . .' Eve stared, then laughed shrilly.

'What are you talking about? I met Peter at the Blakeley's dinner party and——'

'I know you did,' Rydal cut in blandly, 'and the cosy relationship that followed really touched my heart.'

So he had known about it all along. 'But the fact is,' she heard him continuing, 'he *is* a pressman. He's not known as such locally because the whole of the

Caribbean is his picking ground. But he's a man of charm, I'll grant you that. That's why he finds it no trouble extracting dinner invitations, to meet people like you.'

'I don't believe any of it.' Eve felt the tears and the hurt dangerously near to the surface. 'Why would he befriend me just for a story, as you're making out?'

'Probably looking for a different slant on our brand new marriage.' Rydal lifted his big shoulders, a glint in his eyes. 'Maybe he sensed that there was something missing in our honeymoon bliss and wanted to be the first into print with your obliging revelations.'

So it was true! Yes, Eve knew it now. Peter's timing, his knowledge of when Rydal was and was not away from the house, had been too uncannily correct. He had always known when it was safe to drive up openly to the hillside residence to collect her, and when he must drop her off on the curve of the road and leave her to walk the rest of the way, on her return.

She blinked back the tears furiously. Peter, warm and understanding and concerned. How much of his concern had been genuine? How much of his warmth had been for her, not the potential news scoop that he saw in her? That was something that she would never know now. She had clung to him as a friend, found solace in his companionship. And all the while Rydal had known.

This was something else which made her clench her fists to hold back the tears. There were no security men with them on this trip. During their holiday Rydal had repelled the nuisance of the pressmen when necessary, but he had done nothing about the man she had grown foolishly attached to. And now all at once, seeing him standing there she knew why. *He wanted her to suffer as he had suffered by trusting someone who turned out to be ethically unsound.* But he was wrong! Wrong about her! She choked back the harsh dry tears in her throat. Dear

God! Was there no limit to which his cruelty would go to teach her a lesson for what he believed was her trickery!

He was viewing her cryptically, a look she knew so well. That smile too was sickeningly familiar to her. But for all his steely satisfaction, his expression beneath his tan was drawn and as though the episode was best forgotten he stated harshly, 'Our honeymoon has gone on long enough. It's time we went home.'

CHAPTER FOURTEEN

MARTINIQUE, island of humming birds, golden sunsets and palms. Fort-de-France with its French automobiles, *francs* and *centimes*, *gendarmes*, cafés and Parisian-like little shops, yet wholly tropical island atmosphere. Yes it was home to Eve, even though she had known but a fleeting happiness here.

Like any other honeymoon wife she now had to familiarise herself with household routine. As Mrs Rydal Grantham she was mistress of the house screened by banana plantations and tucked away on the wild Atlantic side of the island. She learned gradually to overcome the language difficulty with Lise and Clemane, the housekeeping couple. Though she would never master their sing-song patois she was able to pick out key words, and discovered that they had seen her that night at their home village of Corobrier with *le patron* but had not wanted to interrupt what looked like the first sweet stirrings of *amour*.

At their mutual twinkles Eve felt a knife thrust in her heart. They may well be right. As early on as that she had known that Rydal stirred her as no man had ever done before. But she had had no inkling then of the misery and heartache that was to follow.

The security men were back patrolling the house and grounds. Occasionally on the way down to the beach she would nod to Lazus, the man who had seen her on the harbour front with Rex. She often wondered what he thought of her marriage to his employer amid all the fuss of being discovered. But perhaps he too believed in true love, for his smile was always respectful, his manner pleasant.

She never moved through the house without remembering the macabre tour that afternoon on her first visit when Rydal had learned the truth about her brother. But she was his wife now and free to wander where she pleased. One afternoon when he was away from the house she discovered his work offices in a separate wing of the sealed-in jungle residence.

Knowing his job she was not surprised at the intricacy of the equipment. Much of it was beyond her comprehension, still she wandered around fingering the huge draught-boards and plotting sheets. Switching on one of the poised angle lamps, there was such a mass of detail she wondered how one man's brain could take in anything so vastly complicated.

One whole side of a room was a technical library filled with aircraft manual design texts. There was a modelling table littered with bits of clay, plastic and metal fragments, a computer-desk, a telex console, and in an ante-room furnished with comfortable armchairs, the coffee table was strewn with aeronautics magazines.

Yes, it was clear she was married to a technical genius. Here was Rydal the man of the air. But what of Rydal the husband? She swallowed on the lump in her throat. Would she only ever know his cruelty and ruthlessness? Oh, he was benevolent towards her in the material sense. She had clothes, a lovely home, her own private beach . . . He was even protective, instructing his staff to keep an eye on her at all times. Perhaps he was thinking of her naïveté with Peter Arnwood. Or was this part of her punishment too, being confined to the house and grounds? Yes, Rydal was thoughtful and protective, but never once did he let her forget that she owed him an intolerable debt, and that he intended to extract every last ounce of penitence for her trickery.

She had known the torture would go on, but she was not sure what form it would take until she saw the lovely shape of Philippa Marchant at a dinner party they gave a few days after their return. After that she was left wondering no longer. They gave parties two or three times a week, though Eve knew that Rydal wasn't the party-going type. She was the hostess, but he always made up the guest-list and invariably Philippa's name was on it. Philippa always on Bruno's arm, but provocation in her look, her smile and the way she talked when Rydal was around.

He was discreet. She had to thank him for that. Before the guests he was always the attentive husband. But there were other times when perhaps Philippa was one of the last to leave, and Eve would be wearily taking the night air out on the rear veranda overlooking the beach path and portion of pewter ocean. Then she would see the two shapes at the far end of the veranda in the shadows. Rydal and Philippa in close embrace, his lips locked passionately on hers.

It was a death blow each time she witnessed the scene, yet she had no choice but to go on witnessing it, for there was no hiding from what Rydal chose to make obvious. She would clench her hands until the nails bit deep into her flesh and choke back the tears. To him she was just some cheap deceiver who had married him to save her brother from the noose. He couldn't know that he was breaking her in two with his vindictive displays.

She began to dread the dinner party evenings. While she had grown thinner, paler and more fragile in appearance, Philippa was in the flower of womanhood. She had acquired a golden tan and with her dark beauty she resembled an exotic island flower. Confident of her attraction she was curious and even a little pitying in an amused way where Eve was concerned.

One evening when she had left the lighted front veranda to walk a little way into the garden Philippa caught her up in her dainty high heels. Anyone viewing the gesture from indoors would think they were two close friends getting away from the overall chatter for a while to gossip between themselves. But Eve knew different. Philippa had come to crow.

She found a seat under a flamboyant tree, its flame-like blossom faintly lit by the glow from the veranda. It didn't surprise her when the other woman joined her. They sat for some moments in silence, Philippa pulling lazily on a cigarette as though she was quite content to listen to the sounds of the night. But she was not the sort of person to expand amidst the beauties of nature. It was doubtful if she saw anything but what was in her own mind and it wasn't long before she was opening the inevitable subject with, 'You know, pet, you should never have come to this island. You simply don't belong among us. Oh, I'll admit you play the hostess well. You've acquired a certain poise and you do have this serene air, but you're light-years away in what it takes to be the life and soul of one of these parties.'

'Are you considering giving me lessons?' Eve asked drily and they both knew what she meant by that.

'Believe me I'd like to,' came the husky reply, 'but I'd be wasting my time. As a village Miss you'd never make it. It's something you're born with.'

'The talent for travel or making one's mark on foreign ground?'

'You haven't a bent for either, darling. The first thing we girls do when we come out to our winter playground is to line up who there is to play with.'

'Among the male element of course?'

'What else?'

'I would have thought I'd passed my initiation easily,' Eve said. 'After all I married my playmate.'

'You married him, but is he your mate?' Thick curling lashes were lowered over the lovely violet eyes as Philippa blew smoke leisurely from a sensual coral smile. 'I get the feeling that there's something lacking in your style, darling.'

'Which you're more than willing to fill in with from your own abundant supplies,' Eve murmured, though her chest was tight at the effort of sounding nonchalant.

'As I said, you ought to get back to that country parish of yours. You'd do okay courting the local practitioner or somebody.'

'As a matter of fact,' Eve spoke reminiscently, 'I went out quite a few times with the new village doctor. Jim Paisley. A very nice person.'

'You see what you're missing!' Philippa homed in on this. 'You certainly took a wrong turning when you chose Martinique for a holiday.'

'I gather your own ... er ... conquests would take a little longer to list?' Eve said.

'What do you think, pet?' Throaty laughter accompanied the reply. 'I was born with a silver spoon in my mouth but unfortunately only in the literal sense. I've had to vet the bank vaults of my various boy friends. I mean, you can't live the life of the idle rich without the necessary acoutrements needed to stay a member of the jet-set.'

'And does Bruno finally come up to expectations in that respect?' Eve asked.

'I wouldn't say finally ...' There was a significant pause. 'I seem to have a fatal attraction where the opposite sex are concerned. I mean, I'm fond of Bruno but he is by no means the only suitor in my life.'

'But suitors don't include married men, isn't that right?'

'My suitors, darling, include anyone.'

At the smooth sultry tones Eve asked, 'Isn't Bruno going to get peevish?'

'I can handle Bruno.' The comment was made provocatively; also the advice. 'Maybe you should look to your own home site.'

'I intend to,' Eve said quietly and rose, adding, 'Excuse me, I ought to be getting back to the guests.'

She felt that those attractive violet eyes bored into her back with feline satisfaction as she walked over to the house, and she had to admit she'd made a poor showing against Philippa's husky guile.

Her eyes smarted with unshed tears. Perhaps love made one more vulnerable in such matters. It was easy to reign supreme over a discussion when the emotions were as ice-cool and untroubled as Philippa's were. Fractionally her step faltered and for some reason then she thought of Doris Maton's words. *You have the look of a woman who might break easily under excessive pressure ... I don't want to see you hurt ...*

Was she indeed cracking under the strain? She raised her chin a little. No. She would never do that. She would go through hell and fire to stay at Rydal's side. On the other hand she didn't intend to let him have it all his own way.

It was that same evening when all the guests had finally gone that she broached the subject of Philippa. They were in the master bedroom preparing to retire for the night. Eve slept here while Rydal used the adjoining bedroom but as his things were here she sat in a negligée at the mirror, brushing her hair until he left.

Her insides churning, she said as evenly as she could manage, 'If we go on giving parties at this rate, we're likely to run out of guests to invite.'

'Don't concern yourself with that, my dear,' he said suavely. 'I don't think the lists will run dry yet awhile.'

'No, and there'll always be one guest we can count on, in any case.' She used the hairbrush a little too vigorously.

'I take it you're referring to Philippa.' He smiled, putting it into words for her. And tying the belt of his dressing gown, 'If her presence bothers you, you only have to say so.'

'I don't feel disposed to tittivate your satisfaction with complaints.' She placed the hairbrush down carefully. 'What I can't understand is why you consider me by being discreet about it. If you and Philippa have nothing to hide from me why not go the whole hog and let everybody in on the secret?'

'Could it be you're angling for sympathy in that direction?' he queried mockingly.

'Sympathy for what?' She turned from the dressing table. 'Your shallow behaviour aimed at teaching me a lesson?'

'It does seem to have got under your skin,' he drawled maddeningly.

'That should please you.' Her voice shook despite her efforts to keep it steady.

'Well, well!' He moved to where she sat. 'Do I detect something of the green eye of the little yellow god here?' He jerked her to her feet and hard against him. 'As you know, we can rectify that any time.' His lips sought the hollow of her throat.

Suppressing a shudder of pleasure she returned his barbed smile and replied, 'With your performance these past evenings I wouldn't want you to overtax yourself.'

His grin was as virile as ever but his eyes were tempered steel as he spoke. 'You like to call a spade a spade, don't you, Eve. Pity you couldn't have been so frank when we first met.'

'When we first met I found you every bit as repulsive as your precious guard beasts,' she lied to get the better of him.

'Of course,' he smiled, 'but it was worth it just to get to know me.'

'You've convinced yourself you were something special to me in some way from that first day,' she squirmed. 'I've given up trying to get you to see that yours is a pure case of inflated ego.'

'I've got your type to thank for that.' His grip was unrelenting. 'If I was left in peace instead of being chased all over the globe by your sensation-mongering pals my ego would be right where it belongs, behind my work.'

'That's another fixation you've got.' Somehow they both appeared to have forgotten Philippa. 'I have no newspaper pals as you call them. My brother's a journalist and I made the mistake of agreeing to a stupid plan of his. But I never went through with it. And this will be another blow to that super ego of yours. The last man I wanted to run into at Corobrier that night was you.'

Rydal's gaze was narrow and searching. His fingers sinking into her flesh he murmured at length, 'Oh, you're a clever wench, Eve. It's a good job I'm wise to your tricks. Wise to the fact that you sort of bumped into me on two separate occasions and that you went on being pally despite your . . . er . . . aversion to my company.'

'You're the one who made me stay on at Corobrier,' she flashed. 'And it was you who came to me at the Pension Desirade. I'd spent three days avoiding you.'

His look became distant. He seemed to be thinking over what she had said. His tones however were as metallic as ever as he pointed out, 'But you didn't avoid me when we visited Ignace and his family the following day, or the time we took the trip to the rain forest or . . .' the pause was hatefully significant '. . . the night we sailed on the ferry to Pointe du Bout and danced amid the palms.'

'That,' Eve could feel that she had paled at the very memory, 'was something altogether different.'

'Oh, different, eh?' That probing look again. 'Well that's a new angle. In what way different?'

'I . . . can't explain now.' The steely eyes raked her. How could she speak of love in so untender a moment? His jaw hardened. 'No? Well let me do it for you. Brother Rex was putting on the pressure and the outings were necessary to gain a foothold in my confidence.'

'Rex had nothing to do with my meeting you,' she choked. 'Yes, he was hounding me for information but never at any time did I disclose a word of what you told me.'

'Well, aren't you the true-blue girl-guide!' His satire was unbearable. 'You had nothing to do with brother Rex's beach plan, you were running away from me the night of the festival, you went on plantation outings because of something "different" and you didn't say a dickey-bird to newsman Bowen about our board-meeting conversations!'

'Is it so difficult to understand that I lost my nerve after agreeing to help Rex by meeting up with you again at Corobrier?' she reiterated vehemently while his fingers bruised her flesh. '*I lost my nerve* and ran for the bus and I would have kept on running if you hadn't made it so ... impossible!' Her head had dropped back and she blinked away the tears before re-gathering her strength. 'If you'd come down from that almighty pedestal of yours perhaps you'd see I was telling the truth.'

His face as white as hers, he looked as if he half wanted to. But he would have had to have been a fool to ignore all the damning evidence against her and wearily Eve knew he was no fool.

'Why don't we stop going round in circles with this thing and get back to what we know and understand between us?' He brought his savage smile close. 'If the thought of Philippa gets under your skin why not do something about eliminating the competition?'

'Oh for pity's sake let go of me!' She wrenched herself free of his arms, swept to the door of the connecting room and, their roles reversed, slammed it shut, leaving him to the master bedroom.

Eve slept little that night. She arose in the morning with one thought in her mind. She had to get away from

Rydal. She wasn't thinking of herself now. She had lain awake all through the dark hours and she knew that she must put her feelings to one side where he was concerned. It wasn't her own suffering. It was his. All she had been through she would go through again just to be allowed to stay close to him. But it was what he was doing to himself.

He was not a man who sought the limelight but he gave parties to torment her with his double-edged humour. He didn't love Philippa yet he flirted with her within view of their private rooms, another form of punishment. He had let her make a fool of herself with Peter Arnwood as a way of getting even, and she had had to weather the hostility of his train of female admirers which he had gone out of his way to serve up to her on their pseudo-honeymoon travels.

All this was bad enough for a man whose fame gave him no peace in the news world, but worst of all he was making no move to return to his chosen profession. Rex had said that the French would like him to work for them, so too the Americans. But there had been no French plane-makers permitted to the dinner-parties or for private talks. Nor had the heads of the big aircraft firms in the United States been given an opening to attend.

Obviously Rydal couldn't go on like this. And how could she go on when it was clear she was ruining his career? It was up to her to step out of his life, putting an end to his obsession with her and leaving him free to devote himself once more to the work he loved.

But how to get away? The grounds were watched and the only time she left the house was at Rydal's side in the car. Even if she could seize a car she had no idea what triggered off the mechanical opening device on the gate. No, going the road way was out, so she spent the afternoon weighing up the beach. Under cover of bathing and examining shells she saw that the two headlands closed round the private beach like protective arms. The one she had scaled with Rex's help she could do again. The only snag with this was it was nearer to the property and in full view of the security men. Night time might be an advantage but they were trained to keep an eye on the vulnerable points. Hence the guard dogs they employed. Luckily the canine sentinels were indifferent to her movements now, they had seen her so often on the beach. She might try for the further headland but this had the proportions of a cliff face, so considering it may well be a waste of time.

All in all the position appeared as hopeless as the front of the house. There was however one spark of a possibility which she gave a great deal of thought to while swimming and pottering about on the sand. The pair of veteran Creole gardeners possessed a decrepit boat almost as old as themselves. It was splintered and patched and painted a thick, lumpy slate blue inside and out. With the skimping perseverence of the elderly they had transformed it from a wreck and it looked about as sea-worthy as a wooden cullender, yet they went out at dawn most days and caught fish either for themselves or the household.

Eve had no such ambitious plans in mind. If she could push the boat out from where it was beached about half-way along the crescent of sand, she would stand a better chance of making a getaway unseen on the dark sea than she would attempting the slow haul clambering over loose and easily dislodged rocks. She need only row around the nearest headland a mere matter of yards then she could wave down a car. Once in Fort de France she would decide on the next step for leaving the island.

After the ice-cool planning was over she returned to the house a quivering wreck. It was one thing to make a decision and another to follow it through. Could she wrench herself away from the man she loved so desperately? Could she push behind her the ultimate contentment of knowing she was his wife, albeit in name only? What would be the position if she stayed? With an ache in her heart she knew the answer to that. There was nothing she could do to make him see that she had never cheated him, therefore she must leave him with his anger which would diminish with time.

She was thankful for the darkness which dropped like a blanket a little after six over these windward isles. Dinner was not for another hour or so, so no one would miss her. In her room she put on a pair of dark slacks and a close-fitting top that wouldn't flap around her. It was the sound of the wind which was causing her some concern. Here on the Atlantic side of the island she had seen how the seas could change from a glass-like surface to towering waves in a matter of minutes. The holiday brochures described these shores as wind-lashed and romantic. How romantic would they be, she wondered, when one was steering a boat round a rocky headland in the dark?

The squall was gathering momentum when she got down to the beach. The guard dogs growled suspiciously as she went by, then apparently washed their hands of her, preferring to curl up in their quarters inside the undergrowth. The waves though slight as yet had an oily gleam, suggesting a considerable swell. She was half-torn into postponing her plan, but knew that if she didn't go tonight she would never find the will or the strength to try again. In any case there was nothing dangerous in what she was attempting. She would be round the headland with half a dozen strokes of the oars. And she wasn't new to this kind of activity. She had more than once rowed her aunt on the Ingledene river.

Thick cloud blotted out the star-glow, a fact she was thankful for. And on such a night the risk of security men on the prowl was lessened. With this thought in mind she wondered if she shouldn't make, after all, straight for the headland. But the sound of her picking her way over the rocks would most certainly alert the suspicions of the guard dogs and this was a chance she couldn't afford to take.

The only sign of life distinguishable from the sea's edge was the dim glow from the gardener's shack set some way back in the forest. Their matchwood boat was a lot heavier than it looked when it came to pushing it out. The buffeting winds were no help, but an occasional surge of water which soaked her sandals helped to loosen it from its sandy hold.

She was beginning to feel its buoyancy, had her hands placed on its rough wood bow ready to clamber in when a sound other than that of the fretful breeze made the hairs stand up on the back of her neck. She sensed another presence on the beach, who or what she didn't know . . . a dark shape moving in behind her . . . Perhaps it was one of the guard dogs come to sniff after her departure. She held her breath expecting to hear a throaty growl of distrust. And that was her undoing.

If she had pushed off there and then as she was poised to do, probably nothing would have gone amiss. But hesitating that fraction of a second left her unprepared for the sudden lifting of the boat. It rose in the water with such force it completely unbalanced her, buckling her knees so that she fell forward sprawling headlong into it.

With the rush of the waves and the tumbling of the boat the squall was suddenly all about her. Above the shrieking of the wind she couldn't have said whether that was the barking of a dog or a human shout which followed her from the fast-receding shore.

Bruised and dazed, she grabbed at anything which would help her to attain a sitting position, but the craft, which had stubbornly refused to leave the sand now bobbed on the swell with the lightness of a cork. She felt it rolling and sliding down crests like driftwood so that no sooner had she righted herself to catch a glimpse of brooding sky and rolling dark ocean than she was jolted off balance and sent rattling around the rough interior.

Soaked and gasping for breath she had visions of being swept out to sea. However, after some minutes following the rhythm of the swell she realised that the boat was caught between the suction and tow of the two headlands and might well remain in this position all night, first rushing tantalisingly close to the beach, then careering sea-wards until caught by the incoming waves.

If she could only find the oars. If she could only stay upright long enough to steady the bobbing motion of the craft and aim it for the further beach. Groping frantically her fingers closed round something in the bottom of the boat, but she was never to learn if it had been an oar or not for in that moment a cross-wind hit the stern. The gust sent everything spinning and the next thing she knew she was floundering in deep water with the matchwood craft upturned and slewing dangerously close.

She grabbed it. She could swim, but not this distance from the shore. Perhaps if she hung on the moment would come when she could make it to the beach.

It was like waiting for the pendulum to swing. Waiting, waiting for an ingoing surge which would deposit her close enough to make a try for the shore. She was cold now. The winds had a tropical warmth and the water lapped sluggishly around her aching body, but she was cold with fear. Already spent after her nightmare ride over the waves, she was becoming exhausted now trying to sustain her grip on the nobbly paintwork of the patched-up wreck.

Each time the swell took her a little closer inland, and each time she had to make the fateful decision of whether to make a break for it or whether to hang on. Both choices seemed fraught with danger of some kind.

A particularly heavy swell took her well forward and she was bracing herself for going it alone when a blur of light on the beach distracted her from her purpose. There was noise too and shouts and much activity it seemed. Then a beam of light, a powerful one, came out over the waves. Searchingly it probed the darkness and eventually came to rest on her where she clung to the upturned boat.

She was so near the shore now a few good strokes would have taken her inland, but her limbs had gone stiff at the commotion on the beach, and her heart pounded not just with the effort of staying afloat. She had been found out! Someone had seen her taking the boat out and had given the alarm, or the guard dogs had alerted the security men. Whatever, her plan to leave had been discovered. Even if she made for the beach now she couldn't hope to disappear as she had planned to.

Fixed in the brilliant spotlight she felt like a trapped animal. While she struggled to think what to do next a voice came out over the water. 'Hang on, Eve! I'm coming out!'

Rydal! She went weak at his shout. So he was there too! And she hadn't wanted him to know. Oh dear heaven, what should she do now! Tears mixed with the salt water in her eyes. He mustn't come out here! He mustn't find her! Didn't he know she couldn't stay? Didn't he know she was death to his career? She had to get out of his life—and stay out.

Gathering her strength she lined up her position from the shore. She would have to aim for the far beach beyond the headland. It would mean swimming parallel for a while but in the darkness she could easily dodge the spotlight; also the wind was lessening. The squall which had sprung up suddenly could just as rapidly disperse and the waves were in her favour. She had to avoid Rydal at all costs.

Steeling herself she slackened her grip on her floating support. The water dragged at her limbs without its comforting buoyancy. Just as it had been before it upturned it was a light craft afloat and easily influenced by conflicting currents. This was something she should have remembered, but in her anguish to leave before Rydal found her she saw nothing but the ruin she had caused him. So as she moved off she gave no thought to wind direction or the capriciousness of the waves.

Swimming heavily, she didn't recall being struck on the head by the spinning craft, at the mercy of the swell now without her weight on it. She only knew that she was sinking down and down and down, that it was pleasant not to have to struggle any more. Musing drowsily, it came to her that perhaps this was the best way. This way she would be out of Rydal's life for ever . . .

She floated on the blackness almost happily. With such a glorious feeling of well-being she wanted no part of the turmoil going on about her. Hidden forces would not let her rest. They were pummelling her, tugging her, jolting her from her oh so comfortable cloud. She desisted, clinging to the pleasurable mist, some section of her mind telling her there was pain where she had come from and there would be pain if she went back.

Pain! Suddenly her whole body seemed filled with it. No longer could she drift blissfully detached. Her cloud had become immeasurably inhospitable. Desperately she sought her dream world and knew only a hard and unyielding rack. Weeping a little at what she had lost, the desire to sink into oblivion was stronger than ever.

Perhaps she would never have heeded the demands made on her if it hadn't been for a voice in the misty blackness. An oh so distant voice penetrating to her cold and lifeless heart, warming her very bones with its compassion, rekindling her tears with its tenderness. 'Eve! Eve! For the love of heaven come back to me!

Eve! I love you more than life itself! Speak to me, my darling.'

Speak! She wanted to sing! For Rydal was close, oh so close. She was in his arms in her dream world she was sure, for he had said he loved her. *He loved her!* Just as dreamily she replied, 'I love you too, Rydal. I've always loved you. That's why I was going away.'

'Well that's a cock-eyed statement if ever I heard one!' The deep laughter sounded shaky with a powerful relief, and a little dryness. 'Maybe it has something to do with the knock on the head.'

Yearning to see that beloved craggy face she raised her lashes then. Slowly she became aware that it was no dream. But how could she be sorry when the man who was her husband was gazing down at her with an overwhelming light of love and tenderness in his expression.

'Rydal!' She clung to him. 'You're here!'

'I'll always be here, my love. And never, never do that to me again.'

She stirred in the tightness of his embrace. He was wet. Dripping wet. And so was she. And now she knew why her body ached so. She was lying on the rough wood timbers in the bottom of the boat. Rydal must have righted it. What it must have cost him to steady its lethally swinging motion, search for her in the depths and haul her on board, she could not begin to conceive.

'Lie still,' he soothed close to her ear. 'I've tied a rope on the bow. They're winching us in.'

Nestled in his arms she saw that the clouds above were dispersing and the stars shone in a clear velvet-dark sky. She could feel the strong, swift motion of the boat cutting through the water, somewhat different to her own floundering efforts earlier. Soon the abrupt thud of the sand beneath them brought them to a jerking halt.

Enfolded and transported on to solid ground in

Rydal's arms Eve was bemusedly aware of the commotion on the beach; the machinery, the activity, the men, the searchlight. *All this for her!*

They left it behind as Rydal swiftly carried her towards the beach bungalow. For the first time she viewed it in its clearing without a tightening of her nerves, and indoors it was as though she and Rydal had finally come home.

Along a corridor and into a bathroom area he deposited her under the shower. The water from the tap was warm and inviting. 'Get out of those wet clothes,' she was told. 'I'll make us something hot to drink.'

She was donning a fleecy towelling robe later and shaking out her russet damp hair when Rydal returned. He too was dry and pulsatingly virile in blue beach robe, his hair just springing into life after being towelled and combed. 'Don't try to walk. Here.' He swung her into his arms and retraced his steps along the corridor. In the room with the potted plants and folkweave curtains he set her down on the divan. He would have had her lie like an invalid, but she curled up, allowing him room to lower himself beside her. He drew up the coffee table, holding the two mugs of steaming beverage.

For a long time they sipped in silence. But this new bliss of being together, this heavenly lack of hurry to break the spell, the magic of their togetherness, had to be explained and eventually Rydal asked, 'Perhaps you'd care to tell me now what happened tonight. You almost drowned and you said it was because you loved me. Does your affection for me have that kind of effect on you?'

Their mugs were on the table. At his ironic tones she moved into his arms. 'Oh, Rydal. It does seem a mix up I know,' she twinkled apologetically. 'But I was worried about you.'

'Well, wifely concern at last,' he grinned. 'You were worried about me, so you took off in a storm in a decrepit tub and ended up capsized and knocked senseless.' His voice had hardened and she took his hand and pressed it to her cheek. 'I had to get away from you,' she smiled gravely. 'I was concerned about your work. Before I came into your life the whole world was buzzing with your aircraft designing abilities. You were feted and sought after and written about and everyone was waiting to see what you would do next. I haven't helped at all,' she sighed. 'Your career has become stagnant because of me. That's why I decided you would be better off without me.'

'Let's get this straight.' With a warm finger under her chin he turned her face towards him and looked deep into her eyes. 'You went through all that tonight because you thought I'd turned my back on my profession?'

'Well, haven't you?' She traced the slope of his mouth with a finger tip. 'You haven't talked aircraft in weeks, at least not where I've been. And all these multi-million concerns angling for your services. You haven't given them the time of day.'

'My poor sweet darling.' He gripped her close. 'I might have lost you . . . I ought to have told you . . .'

'Told me what?' she asked curiously, laughingly stifled by the fierceness of his embrace.

Once again he held her away from him and looked into her eyes. 'Do you remember that afternoon on Mount Pelee when you asked me if I'd come to a decision?'

'About your work?' she nodded. Would she ever forget those poignant moments when she had thought she would be leaving, never to see him again.

'Not just about my work,' he smiled, putting an arm round her shoulder and drawing her head down to rest on his. 'I'd decided about you too. I couldn't very well talk of marriage when we had known each other a mere three weeks. But I was going to ask you to stay on and work my way round to a proposal after a decent lapse of time.'

So he had loved her even then. Eve's heart glowed. Oh the trials of convention. What would it have mattered, three weeks, three days! If only he had spoken to her of his love that memorable afternoon on Mount Pelee.

'My job came secondary to you,' he went on. 'But I'd worked out a scheme which pleased me and which I considered would give us the best life together . . . here on the island.'

'On Martinique!' Eve's heart leapt, but she raised her head to search his face. 'That wouldn't be possible . . . would it?'

'It's more than possible, it's a fact,' he smiled. 'My decision that day was to become a general consultant. That means I'm not tied to any one firm, or to be more exact I'm finished altogether with commercial considerations. Consulting for governments is considerably higher up the scale than what I've been doing. At one swoop it puts me above all the managing directors and chairmen. So you see I haven't been as idle as you think.'

At his hard satisfaction she looked up at him in wonder. 'You haven't indeed. Is that what all the equipment and drawing boards and gadgets is about in your office den?'

He nodded. 'I can do most of the work at home. Occasionally I may have to liaison for Saudi Arabia or Canada or Mexico. It will mean we'll have to travel for about two months in the year. Will you mind that?'

'How could I mind anything with you?' She snuggled against him.

His hand caressing her bath-robed shoulder, he murmured, 'I married you because I couldn't bear to be without you, do you know that?'

'I married you for the same reason,' she confessed softly.

'From the moment I saw your frightened face after we called off those cursed guard dogs I had trouble getting you out of my mind,' he mused aloud, reminiscently. 'After our night together at the village festival you had become a fixture under my skin. I knew I had to see you again. I finally gave up fighting a losing battle with myself and drove over to the Pension Desirade. You weren't in and I wanted to throttle the desk clerk,' he grinned. 'But I hung around and kept my cool, but only just.'

'You think you suffered!' she scoffed softly. 'That night after Corobrier I couldn't sleep for thinking about you. When you came and invited me out for a drive, wild horses wouldn't have kept me away.'

He rubbed his chin against her cheek. 'Old Ignace knew what was going on in my mind.' Taking his lips through her hair he went on musing aloud. 'He said to me, "Son, I'm seventy years old and I'm not a poor man, but I'd trade it all to go back to when I first met Monique".'

'I'd like to have heard that in French,' she smiled dreamily. 'Must have sounded very poetic.'

'Very.' Rydal turned her face his way and kissed her long and tenderly on the lips. His gaze soaking up every nuance of her pale but radiant features he murmured, 'Everything about you is poetic, Eve.' He continued to gaze at her. 'That time down on the beach from Ignace's place, I wanted to kiss you like this. Your hair was blowing in the wind. You looked adorable.'

'I remember that morning,' she dreamed aloud. 'We went to watch the fishermen and we saw a name on one of the children's logs—Summer Swallow.'

Rydal's eyes were still dancing around her lips. 'There were so many times I wanted to kiss you I've lost count—On the wild headland with the colourful cacti growing about you. Certainly on Mount Pelee. I felt like hell not being able to take you in my arms up there in the clouds.'

Eve laughed softly, happily and lay her cheek against his chest. 'Do you know what I can remember most—with love?' she confessed shyly. 'The night we took the ferry to Pointe de Bout and danced the beguine. The Cole Porter song has haunted me ever since. I feel that it's our song in a way, though I'm not too familiar with all the words.' She lifted her shy gaze. 'May we go back there and dance under the stars again?'

'Every night of the week,' he laughed, though his eyes were grave as he added, 'it's a very special memory of mine too.'

They sat contentedly in the glow of a single lamp, letting their thoughts drift. At last Eve said soberly, 'How will I be able to face the household after what I did tonight?'

'Everybody thinks it was an accident,' Rydal informed her. 'Joseph, one of the gardeners, had come down to the beach. He was worried about the boat in the wind and had decided to hoist it on higher ground out of reach of the water. He saw you fall into the boat, and I told him you often took a stroll before dinner. You'd probably seen the boat near the waves and tried to do something about it on your own and had a mishap.'

Hearing this, Eve knew a surge of relief. 'It wasn't my intention to cause all that fuss,' she said in a small voice.

His hand was resting on her shoulder and his fingers gripped her with almost bruising intensity. 'When Joseph ran in to tell me what had happened I thought I'd go out of my mind with worry,' he said tightly. 'I drummed up every man around here and every piece of equipment I could think of for the job.'

'It certainly didn't have the appearance of a private beach when I arrived back,' she put in succinctly.

'It's going to do from now on,' he smiled. 'As a staid old consultant the pressmen are not going to be interested in me any more. We won't be needing security men, guard dogs. We'll just keep the Creole couple to look after us.'

'Will they cope with all the entertaining we've been doing lately?' she asked with a sideways look at him.

He grimaced. 'No more parties,' he said. 'We might have dinner guests occasionally but only close friends. I want you to myself from now on.'

'And Philippa?' she fingered the fleecy lapel of his robe.

'Let's say she evened things up between us after Arnwood,' he glinted down at her.

So he had been eaten up with jealousy at her friendship with Peter just as she had been made miserable by his flirting with Philippa. Well, yes, it was a fair balance she decided happily.

'In any case you won't be seeing Philippa again,' Rydal was saying. 'It seems that Bruno has become impatient with her dithering. He's flying home tomorrow to Papá and the Massaretti oil kingdom. He's given her an ultimatum. Either she accompanies him or she stays behind—for good. If I know Philippa,' Rydal tacked on with a shrewd gleam, 'she'll be on that plane.'

Contentedly Eve rested against him. After a long moment she said, back in a dreamy frame of mind, 'If only Rex knew what he was starting when he brought me out to Martinique.'

Rydal straightened a little where he sat. 'Your brother's due to make a call on us shortly,' he said. 'I told him to withhold my decision about the consultancy until I gave the word. He's probably itching to get it into print.'

'We'll go to the airport and meet him when he comes,' she said impulsively. 'Show him what a happily married couple we are.'

Rydal's arms had lowered. 'I doubt whether you'll be up to such excitement so early after your near drowning.' There was concern in his tones yet Eve felt an ice-cold draught round her heart. 'But we will go back to dance the beguine at Pointe du Bout?' she asked, viewing him anxiously.

'Of course,' he smiled. 'But first I want you thoroughly looked over by the doctor to satisfy myself you've suffered no permanent injury from that crack on the head. At the least, he'll probably recommend several days rest.'

He fingered the dark bruise near her temple with a keen eye then rose and gathered her into his arms. 'It's time you got some rest,' he suggested, 'so it's bed for you, Mrs Grantham, until the doc gives you the all clear.'

Her head resting on his shoulder, Eve's averted gaze was self-questioning as she followed their route through the darkness back to the glow of the veranda and then indoors through the trees.

Rydal transported her with care. He was gentle, compassionate and loving. So why did she feel that the bubble had burst, that the magic had dispersed with the mention of Rex's name?

CHAPTER FIFTEEN

THE foliage surrounding the back lawn was jungle-like. There were orchids here of brilliant hues, flaming poinsettia, the sunshine yellow flowers of the poinciana, while the bamboo formed veritable cathedrals. The wild stretches vibrated with colour, scents and sounds; the droning of insects and croaker lizards, the whistle of tree frogs.

Reclining on her lounger on the veranda, Eve had become familiar with every aspect of the scenery here these past days. She had watched yellow-breasted bananaquits swooping around the tender nests of ferns, ruby-topaz humming birds hovering on the air and butterflies with vivid wings busying themselves above the hanging blossom.

The stiffness in her limbs had receded. The bruises after her battle with the boat had disappeared, and she was no longer dogged by appalling headaches. In fact, apart from a persistent lethargy, she was fit and well. It was only her heart that was still raw, still yearning to be whole, to be complete in its love. Her head resting back among gay cushions she watched a pair of turtle-doves on a nearby branch, with misted eyes. No, her heart hadn't healed. She doubted now if it ever would.

A footstep sounded from indoors. It would be Rydal with their morning coffee tray. He usually left off his work about this time and came to join her for a break.

He carried the tray out and placed it between their two chairs then he bent to drop a kiss on her cheek. 'How's the patient this morning?' He smiled down at her, and big and relaxed in cream shirt and slacks, a

176

cravat tied casually at his throat, the sight of him went
straight to that ache that was her heart.

'I'm no longer an invalid,' she laughed. 'I even took a
turn round the lawn this morning and later I'm thinking
of going further afield.'

'That's what I like to hear.' He poured for them both,
sweetened and milked her coffee just as she preferred it
and handed it to her, his blue eyes whimsical. There was
love there, there was no mistaking that. 'If you fancy
some company,' he put a spoon in his own cup, 'I could
leave off what I'm doing and take a walk with you.'

'And drag you away from your work?' she tilted a
reprehending eyebrow. 'I wouldn't dream of it ...
although I might pass by your windows later and peek
in for a moment.' With a mischievous light she sipped
her coffee. And as she drank she swallowed her sadness.

What more could she ask than this? Rydal loved her
deeply. She loved him with equal fervour. As a married
couple they shared a common bliss. But there was
something missing. And she knew now, had known for
some days, the reason for this cold draught round her
heart. Rydal believed that she loved him, but he didn't
believe that there had been no ulterior motive in her
getting to know him. He would never believe that. They
might live in the fullness of marriage, sharing a life
which had all the indications of being a perfect one, but
there would always be this distance between them, this
echo of distrust which could cloud the day and weight
the spirits with its very tenuousness.

'Joseph tells me he's found a pet for you,' Rydal
refilled their cups. 'It's a mongoose. He's making a pen
for it.'

'I hope he keeps it securely closed in,' Eve was wryly
humorous.

'Don't be too hard on the old boy.' The blue eyes
were also humorous. 'He feels kind of responsible for
you, as it was his boat that gave you a battering.'

'I'm glad to know his tub stood up to the ducking better than I did,' she smiled. And thoughtfully, 'Maybe he'll take me out fishing in it one morning.'

'I hardly think we'll risk that again,' Rydal said drily. 'But as permanent old-timers here now, we might get a sailing craft ourselves. If there's any fishing to be done I'll be at the wheel. And I rather fancy taking you for a sail at sundown. On a calm evening the views above and below the surface hereabouts are somewhat spectacular.' He drank up and rose. 'For now, time to get back to the draught-board. And don't forget, take it easy if you're going away from the house.'

'Nonsense,' she rose too to show him how fit she was. 'I could walk a mile. And remember you promised to take me on the ferry to Pointe du Bout.'

'So I did.' He had put his arms about her waist and drawn her close but she sensed a tightening in him. 'Well, we'll see how you make out for the rest of the day.' He brushed his lips lingeringly against hers and went indoors.

Eve stood motionless for some time. She felt the familiar feathering of a chill over her skin. Why couldn't he bring himself to dance with her again under the Pointe du Bout stars? Had he convinced himself grimly that this was a memory best forgotten? He had said that it was a night precious to him too. But in his mind was it also tainted with distrust?

She walked slowly along the path towards the beach bungalow. The air was filled with the chirping of grasshoppers, the unending trills of crickets and insects. In the bungalow, she wandered through the rooms following the route that Rydal had taken with her in his arms the night of the storm. But there were no signs of the pools their dripping bodies had made; nothing to indicate that bliss of their togetherness here on the divan. Lise had long since been and cleaned up in here and to Eve it was as though the magic of that night had been wiped away along with the disorder.

She found herself wishing fervently that one could go back, that they could go back to those moments in the old tub of a boat when Rydal had held her close and beseeched her not to leave him; to answer him. She wished they could have stayed fixed in that moment of time, their love suspended like some beautiful object embalmed in a glass instead of having to go on contending with reality and all its disillusionments.

She turned her steps towards the outdoors and the beach. Balmy trade winds caressed her cheeks, lifted strands of her hair. The sea was satin calm, wavelets a mere ripple on the pale sand. The sun was warm, everything shimmering; coconut trees, tall ferns, multi-coloured blossoms. Strange how she herself could feel chilled with the glow of the day and the loveliness of the landscape bringing an ache to her throat.

She walked and examined shells, shaded her eyes to linger over distant views, and watched the sea birds nesting in the headland rocks. She was over by the undergrowth viewing the plant life when Rydal showed up on the beach. Her hopes leapt so painfully she had to blink a dampness from her eyes. Had he changed his mind about their night out in Pointe du Bout? Had he come to tell her that they would dance the beguine together amid the palms, after all?

He strolled across the sand his arms outstretched. He took her hands in his and his eyes had lost none of their love. He was even lazily hospitable as he explained the reason for his trip out here. 'Rex is on the island. He's just rung from the airport. I told him we'd wait lunch until he arrived.'

Rex. Her brother Rex, who also believed she had done as he asked when he had wanted information on his aircraft designer. Rydal hadn't suggested that they drive out to the airport to pick him up. And she was glad now. There wouldn't have been much point in demonstrating to her brother what a happily married couple they were she smiled bleakly to herself. Rex's mind centred solely around his work, and he was only coming to the island to secure Rydal's permission to print his decision to go solo in the field of aeronautics.

'That's fine,' she replied now to the news. 'In a taxi he shouldn't be long crossing the island.'

'I'll go and get Lise to add something typical to the menu,' Rydal said. 'Coming?'

'No, I'll stay and gather some flowers for the table.' She watched him return towards the house. How odd that they should both want to make some special effort for Rex's visit. But then, without him Eve would never have come to Martinique.

A mere ten miles by road was nothing in a car. She was still dawdling over the flowers when another figure appeared on the beach. Rex! He trudged smilingly towards her. She was amazed at the difference in him since she had seen him last. He had filled out, got more bulk to his physique. His face was fleshier and in an executive-type suit he exuded an air of success.

'How's my married sister, then?' He hugged her briefly and held her away from him. 'Rydal told me you were out here. He said you'd been a bit under the weather. Something about a capsized boat.'

'Oh I simply got wet,' she smiled. 'I'm fine now. How's the job?'

'It's no longer a *job*, sweetheart,' he winced at her expression. 'Now we're talking of *position*.' He seemed to swell in the sunshine. 'Thanks to you I'm now what we call on *top* of the heap.'

Thanks to her. It was her turn to wince inwardly. Did he have to put into words what everybody was trying to forget around here? 'And you haven't done too bad for yourself either,' he grinned. 'Like I said before, money to burn and a paradise island for a home.' He glanced around him but Eve knew that none of the beauty registered on him. He belonged in a city environment, amisdt office blocks and teeming communities, where there were goals to be aimed for, and where success meant something.

'Hey, I'm famished!' He took her arm. 'Let's go back and eat. Rydal said I was to tell you that lunch is about to be served.'

They walked back arm in arm. For the moment Eve had two men in her life. A husband who was almost everything she could wish for. And a brother whom she still cared for in spite of his egoistic traits responsible for that precious missing link in their marriage.

She arranged in a vase, the flowers she had picked and freshened up before the mirror in her room. She was wearing a sleeveless cream dress with a slender belt at the waist and full skirt. She changed her sandals for a pair of pale medium-heeled shoes and ran a comb through her hair. The sea winds had put a touch of pink in her cheeks. At least there was no outward sign of the languishing wife about her.

The flowers provided a pretty splash of colour on the lunch table. It was almost a gay meal made typical at Rydal's request by the presence of pink lobsters on a platter. These were followed by turtle soup topped with a floating turtle egg, king fish, tiny french loaves, creamed chicken and rice, a green salad, light french pastries and black coffee.

Rex talked all the way through the meal. 'Can't stay on I'm afraid,' he told his hosts while forking up white lobster meat. 'Got to get on to the States by this evening. I'm going great guns there you know. That profile I did on Rydal was syndicated from coast to coast . . .'

'. . . The T.V. moguls were on to me as soon as I smashed into print with that story,' he expanded over the creamed chicken. 'I sifted through the offers and

I've been doing a stint as a newscaster. You know, a kind of T.V. presenter who interviews leading personalities. That sort of thing . . .'

'I've zipped back and forth across the Atlantic in the Concorde like taking a bus,' he laughed between mouthfuls of french pastry. 'Apparently the American audiences are going cuckoo over my appearances. English accent and all that. The television company's been paying my fare but I've become such a hot property there's pressure for me to make my home in the States.'

Eve sipped her coffee. It wasn't that long ago that Rex was regarding Rydal as a 'hot property'. It would be ironic if *he* ended up being hounded by newsmen eager for a new slant on *his* rise to fame. She had no humour in her to appreciate the irony. Also the conversation had to be kept smoothly flowing, for although Rex monopolised it, it was considered polite by the Granthams to fill him in on their honeymoon tour, the people they had met *en route* and the places they had visited.

So much had been said all round that it was well into the afternoon when they retired to the outdoors for a relaxing drink. The gardens at the front of the house were park-like in their immensity. The thick forests of trees surrounding the lawns were now superfluous for their privacy. And there were no longer any security men patrolling behind the scenes. They still had Joseph and his assistant, the two old gardeners to keep things trim, and Lise and her husband to run the house, but there was a delicious feeling of freedom without those well-meaning presences lurking out of sight. And the guard dogs, so she had heard, were living in semi-retirement with Lazus in his house in Fort de France.

Rex and Rydal smoked on the front veranda and drank their after lunch liquor companiably. Eve enjoyed the perfume of the flowers; in fact all the scents

that were rife in the air on Martinique. The spices, the
tang of wild coffee, the distinctive herbs, the banana
flower and the earthy fragrance from the plantations.
On the breeze she caught the redolence of cane juice
simmering and she remembered . . .

It seemed hours later that she came back from her
reverie, from the pain of nostalgia, to hear Rex saying,
'I'll probably settle for a house in the States.'

'You could do worse,' Rydal opined, pulling lazily on
his cigarette.

'New York's the place to be these days. The
pressure's terrific but I thrive on it. I reckon that's
where I'll end up.'

'We can drop in and see you when we're up that
way.'

Rex turned to look at the other man. His face rosy
with the meal and drink he said expansively, 'You know,
I think that's right neighbourly of you. Considering
what Eve and I did to you, you've been big-hearted
about the whole affair. Makes me feel a bit of a chiseller
now, pulling that banana path stunt.'

'Sure, the banana path stunt,' Rydal gulped on his
drink vaguely.

'Don't tell me you don't remember!' Rex was mildly
disappointed that his slick plan hadn't made a more
lasting impression. 'I thought it showed a touch of
mastery the way I organised it, that oh so casual
running into each other,' he grinned. 'Eve starting out
from the square, and you coming in from the beach. God
it must have been a peachy meeting right there among the
rocks!'

Rydal put his glass down carefully. 'You know old
man,' he said with an odd look on his face, 'I am a bit
hazy on that night. . . . Can you . . .sort of freshen it in
my mind?'

And vain as always Rex smiled with injured pride,
'It's not very flattering to know that the V.I.P. coup of

the century is now just water under the bridge. It was that split-second timing that gave it that touch of genius. Eve caught the—what was it?—four o'clock bus which got her to Corobrier about three quarters of an hour later. I knew you'd be on the beach dais at five handing out the prizes, and I knew you'd start off for the village square at exactly five-thirty . . . checked it all out you see.' His grin showed no sign of sheepishness. 'That's the beauty of these security-proof programmes, everything's timed to go like clockwork. No guesses as to where I got the information by the way. A journalist is not obliged to disclose his source remember. Anyway all I had to do was stress on Eve that she had to be on her way to the beach at five-thirty prompt. She couldn't miss. Right there on the banana path she had to run smack into you. Oh it was a master stroke all right! It must have gone like a dream.'

'Yes . . . it went like a dream . . .' Rydal said distantly. 'And you're right. It was . . . a peachy meeting.' Pale but smiling he pushed his glass further on to the table then he rose abruptly. 'Look, old boy, do you mind if we break this up now? I mean, isn't it time you were making for the airport?'

Rex blinked. 'I'm not in that much of a rush . . . I'd planned to stay for dinner . . .'

'Sorry, old man, we're going out,' Rydal was looking about him. 'You can . . . er . . . catch an earlier plane can't you?'

'Well I suppose I could . . . but what about transport? I was rather hoping you'd . . .'

'Ah, here's your bag,' Rydal brought it out from inside the doorway. 'That's everything I think, isn't it?' He took Rex's arm and lifted him out of his seat. 'Look. I'll tell you what. Why don't you take my car? We can pick it up later at the airport.'

'All right,' Rex went with him towards the veranda steps a little dazed. 'But what about this consultancy decision? We were going to talk it over remember. I mean ... do I get the all clear?'

'Print what you like. You have my blessing. Now here are my car keys,' Rydal ushered him on to the drive. 'And here's my car. I'll stow your luggage for you ... like so ... and away you go.'

As he was marched towards the driving seat Rex threw his glance to the sky and said with a lopsided grin, 'These honeymoon couples!' He watched as the door was closed decisively on him and starting up he called laconically through the open window, 'So long you two. And I hope on my next visit I get to make the evening meal.'

Rydal had Eve in his arms before the car had disappeared out of the drive gates. 'My poor angel,' he held her tightly. 'Can you ever forgive me? I've been a swine to you.'

Smothered by his kisses Eve began to feel now that the pain had been worth it. Any ordinary man who thought he had been cheated would have been angry certainly, but after giving a piece of his mind to the woman in question he would quickly have put the episode behind him. But a man in love would not forget. He would want to hurt back, and now she could feel that the more the hurt she had suffered at Rydal's hands the stronger had his love been for her.

Yes, a love like that was worth the rough ride, she half-laughed to herself with delirious happiness.

When she had a free moment from his lips she spoke softly, 'Everything pointed towards my guilt. And you've made up for it these past days.'

'I want to make up for it more.' He caressed her throat, her ears, her hair with his lips. 'We'll have a second honeymoon. Just the two of us. I'll show you the splendour of the sunsets in our cruising jet and we'll limit our stays to desert islands.'

Coming up for air she cast him an amused twinkle.

'You call yourself a staid old consultant! Those don't sound to me the designs of someone past their prime, and,' she thrilled at a particularly long and lingering kiss, 'your behaviour at the moment is not exactly staid.'

Slackening his hold fractionally he grinned down at her, big and virile and gentle, 'Oh, Eve, I love you. I want to tell you that every day of my life.'

Eve rested in his arms knowing that she wouldn't need to hear it. Rydal had proved to her that his love was strong enough to see them into eternity. And her own, no less a force, would endure beside his.

As they stood there on the drive, in the sunshine, amid the green lawns, trailing blossoms and jewelled birds, Rydal's lips began to twitch. 'I was thinking,' he said, his brow crinkling with humour, 'We'll have to take Lise and Clemane's old jalopy when we go out tonight. Me in my evening get-up and you in that silver dress of yours, we're going to look like a couple of broken-down swells driving into town.'

'I wouldn't care if we went in a go-cart,' Eve said, her eyes shining.

'Me neither,' he smiled. And his arm about her waist, 'Let's go and book the table right now, we'll insist on the same table, nothing less. And don't forget you'll want your wrap for the ferry.'

Eve walked with him, the tune already trilling in her mind *I'm with you once more under the stars . . .*

Once more, her heart sang, and always, with Rydal.

WORLDWIDE LIBRARY IS YOUR TICKET TO ROMANCE, ADVENTURE AND EXCITEMENT

Experience it all in these big, bold Bestsellers—Yours exclusively from WORLDWIDE LIBRARY WHILE QUANTITIES LAST

To receive these Bestsellers, complete the order form, detach and send together with your check or money order (include 75¢ postage and handling), payable to WORLDWIDE LIBRARY, to:

In the U.S.	**In Canada**
WORLDWIDE LIBRARY	WORLDWIDE LIBRARY
Box 52040	P.O. Box 2800, 5170 Yonge Street
Phoenix, AZ	Postal Station A, Willowdale, Ontario
85072-2040	M2N 6J3

Coming Next Month in Harlequin Romances!

2749   A MATTER OF MARNIE   Rosemary Badger
Convincing an Australian construction tycoon that his
grandmother has been neglected is a formidable task. Living with
him in order to care for the woman is an even greater challenge.

2750   THE PERFECT CHOICE   Melissa Forsythe
A voice student in Vienna seldom turns men's heads. So when a
handsome stranger woos her, she's in too deep by the time she
discovers his motive for choosing her over her beautiful friend.

2751   SAFE HARBOUR   Rosalie Henaghan
This trustworthy secretary weathers her boss's changeable moods
until his woman friend predicts an end to Anna's working days—
and sets out to make her prophecy come true.

2752   NEVER THE TIME AND THE PLACE   Betty Neels
The consulting surgeon at a London hospital disturbs his ward sister's
natural serenity. She's having enough trouble coping with a broken
engagement without having to put up with his arrogance.

2753   A WILL TO LOVE   Edwina Shore
That the family's Queensland homestead should be sold is
unthinkable. But the only way to save it—according to her
grandfather's will—is to marry the same man who rejected her
four years ago.

2754   HE WAS THE STRANGER   Sheila Strutt
The manager of Milk River Ranch knew that a male relative would
inherit her uncle's spread. But why did the beneficiary have to be a
writer who would either sell out or take over completely?

What readers say about Harlequin romance fiction...

"I absolutely adore Harlequin romances! They are fun and relaxing to read, and each book provides a wonderful escape."
—N.E.,* Pacific Palisades, California

"Harlequin is the best in romantic reading."
—K.G.,* Philadelphia, Pennsylvania

"Harlequins have been my passport to the world. I have been many places without ever leaving my doorstep."
—P.Z.* Belvedere. Illinois

"My praise for the warmth and adventure your books bring into my life."
—D.F.,*Hicksville, New York

"A pleasant way to relax after a busy day."
—P.W.,* Rector. Arkansas

*Names available on request.

What the press says about Harlequin romance fiction...

"When it comes to romantic novels...
Harlequin is the indisputable king."
—*New York Times*

"...always with an upbeat, happy ending."
—*San Francisco Chronicle*

"Women have come to trust these
stories about contemporary people,
set in exciting foreign places."
—*Best Sellers*, New York

"The most popular reading matter of
American women today."
—*Detroit News*

"...a work of art."
—*Globe & Mail*, Toronto

Can you keep a secret?

You can keep this one plus 4 free novels

You're invited to accept 4 books and a surprise gift Free!

Acceptance Card

Mail to: **Harlequin Reader Service**®

In the U.S.
2504 West Southern Ave.
Tempe, AZ 85282

In Canada
P.O. Box 2800, Postal Station A
5170 Yonge Street
Willowdale, Ontario M2N 6J3

YES! Please send me 4 free Harlequin Presents® novels and my free surprise gift. Then send me 8 brand new novels every month as they come off the presses. Bill me at the low price of $1.75 each ($1.95 in Canada) — an 11% saving off the retail price. There are no shipping, handling or other hidden costs. There is no minimum number of books I must purchase. I can always return a shipment and cancel at any time. Even if I never buy another book from Harlequin, the 4 free novels and the surprise gift are mine to keep forever.   108 BPP-BPGE

Name _____ (PLEASE PRINT) _____

Address _____ Apt. No. _____

City _____ State/Prov. _____ Zip/Postal Code _____

This offer is limited to one order per household and not valid to present subscribers. Price is subject to change.   ACP-SUB-1